HOLIDAY SECRETS

SUSAN SLEEMAN

HARLEQUIN® LOVE INSPIRED® SUSPENSE

Recycling programs
for this product may
not exist in your area.

LOVE INSPIRED BOOKS

ISBN-13: 978-0-373-45749-6

Holiday Secrets

www.Harlequin.com

Printed in U.S.A.

Then you will know that I am the Lord;
those who hope in Me will not be disappointed.
—Isaiah 49:23

For all the families waiting for their prodigal son
or daughter to return home.

Acknowledgments

A special thank-you to Amanda Williams
for naming Kendall's horse Beauty.
To Leslie McKee for naming Gavin's horse Lightning.
And to Lizzi Rizzi for naming Lexie's horse Misty.
Your help was greatly appreciated!

ONE

Lexie Grant's father had to pick today, of all days, to come back from the dead.

"Not a word from you in over a month." She glanced at his prop plane rumbling in the distance on the abandoned airstrip, the winds from a blue norther howling across the field. "I thought you had to be dead."

"Why in the world would you think that?" Her father raised his chin in his usual haughty manner.

"Your house and office. They were ransacked. Then you go missing. The sheriff couldn't find you, and he suspected foul play. What else was I supposed to think?" She sighed and wished her father cared enough about her and her fourteen-year-old brother, Adam, to have told them he was leaving town. "Where have you been?"

He stepped closer to the crumbling maintenance building shielding them from the harsh wind racing through the Texas Hill Country. "There's no time to explain. I have another appointment and have to leave."

Right. Leave. He'd left her and Adam to be raised by their mother's sister, Ruth, when their mother died giving birth to Adam. Why should Lexie expect him to stay and give her an explanation?

"So why are you here, then?"

"To give you this." He held out a large manila envelope, his hand trembling.

She watched him for a moment, trying to determine if he was shaking from the twenty-five-degree temperature drop in the last hour or if it was more. He stood strong as usual, but something was off. Maybe something to do with his disappearance.

Thankfully, her fears for his safety had been unfounded, and he was alive. Tears of gratitude sprang to her eyes, surprising her, what with their troubled relationship.

He shook the envelope. "Take it."

She might be glad he was alive, but she wanted nothing from him. Nothing at all. She shoved her hands into her pockets.

"The envelope." He glanced over his shoulder to make a furtive sweep of the area.

"If you're worried that someone is watching us, I should tell you Gavin is coming out here to meet me. He needed to talk to me tonight, too."

"You're meeting your old boyfriend? Here? Tonight?" His voice rose as he cut his gaze over the towering copse of bald cypress trees shadowing the abandoned property.

"Yes," she replied, trying not to think about seeing the man she'd once thought she'd spend the rest of her life with, before he'd bailed on her three years ago.

"He's FBI now... I can't... I have to go." He waved the envelope. "C'mon, take it. Everything you need to know is inside. It's insurance to make sure you're safe."

"Safe? Why wouldn't I be safe?"

He opened his mouth to respond but a rumbling noise sounded from the far side of the field, taking his attention.

A dirt bike burst from the shadows and raced straight for them.

"Gavin?" her father asked.

"No. He's riding over on his horse."

"Take this. Now!" Panic wove through his tone. He shoved the envelope toward her.

She'd never seen the all-knowing doctor this rattled. Should she be afraid, too?

"Now!"

She reached for the envelope. He let go, but she didn't have it in hand. The wind whipped it into the air.

"No!" He charged after the envelope dancing toward his plane.

As a pilot, he could jump in the cockpit and take off anytime he wanted, but he seemed more concerned about getting the envelope.

"Are you coming back or leaving?" she called after him.

He didn't respond. She stepped away from the building to get a better look. He charged ahead, then froze in place, staring at the bike rumbling closer. He suddenly bent to grab the envelope. A gunshot rang out, cutting through the night.

Was it the biker? Was he the one shooting at them?

Her father took off, running toward the plane. The bike veered right, bearing down on him. He'd barely made it a few feet when another shot split the air. Then another. Her father went down.

Dad! No! She opened her mouth to scream.

No. Stop. The shooter will hear you. Maybe come after you.

She clamped a hand over her mouth as panic raced along her nerves. What should she do?

Hide. Yes, hide. Now!

She slipped behind the building. Held her breath. Fought the panic. Her horse Misty, tethered a few feet behind her, nervously shifted. Lexie raced to the mare.

"Shh, girl. Don't give me away." She scrubbed her hand down the mare's velvety nose until she calmed. "What do I do, girl? I can't just leave Dad out there."

But could she do otherwise and not be shot?

She had to try. She couldn't lose him when she'd just gotten him back. She was an ER nurse, after all, and she was sure she could help.

Hoping the shooter hadn't seen her, Lexie left the horse behind and peeked around the corner. The biker roared close and came to a stop ten feet from her father. The biker sat there, his gun outstretched, his bike idling. Her father didn't move.

"Stupid old man," the biker yelled as he dismounted.

Gun waving, he strode toward her father.

Was he going to shoot her dad again? Should she intervene or would he shoot her, too?

She had to do something, but if she died, she'd be of no help to anyone. So she had to be careful. Smart. Assess the situation before acting.

She crept around the back of the building. *Good.* Dark shadows clung to the crumbling siding. She eased through the inky blackness. Not only did she have an improved view of the action now, but she would also have a better chance to offer aid if the opportunity presented itself.

The bike's engine cut out and died, but the dying motor only stopped the biker for a second as he paused to look back. He shrugged and continued walking, holding out his gun in a gloved hand. He poked her father's side with a pointy boot. Her father's tortured moan rose into the stark night.

Yes! He's alive!

"Stupid, stupid man," the gunman said. "Running when bullets were flying."

The shooter was tall. Over six feet. Thin. Lexie searched the darkness for his face, but his tinted helmet hid his features. She'd never heard his voice before, but he had a deep Southern accent, so he could be from around their rural Texas county.

He kicked her father again. "You didn't actually think I'd let you meet with the head of the syndicate today, did you?"

The syndicate? Her dad mumbled something, but she couldn't make out his response. She desperately wanted to know what type of trouble her father had gotten into. Even more, she wanted this man to take off so she could tend to her father's injuries.

"You should have known I'd never let you bring me down," the shooter continued. "Not when I'm facing three strikes. I'm not going to prison again and never coming out. You're a smart man. How come you don't know by now that I'm smarter than you? That I'd hunt you down?"

A sick laugh rolled from his mouth and he moved closer.

Lexie held her breath. Waited for a fatal shot to sound.

Instead, the gunman jerked the envelope from her dad's hand and peered around. "So, who's meeting you here tonight?"

Lexie strained to hear the answer.

"No one," her father said, his tone weak and wavering. If she didn't get to him soon, he might not make it. "Was just hiding the envelope. That's all. I swear."

The shooter bent down and pressed the gun against her father's forehead.

Lexie almost gasped but caught herself in time.

The shooter waved the envelope in her father's face. "Thanks for this. I also have the copy you left with your attorney in Mexico. You should never have given him the information. Now he's dead."

"No."

"Yes." His voice was calm, like committing murder was an everyday occurrence for him. "You obviously planned to hand this over to someone tonight. Who?"

"No one," her father insisted.

"Not even your precious Lexie?"

Wait—the shooter knew her name? Knew who she was? Did he know her father was meeting her here? Would he come after her next?

Her heart stammered and panic ricocheted through her.

"Well, old man?" he demanded. "Lexie. Is she meeting you here?"

"No. I was hiding it. In the building. Would've called her later. Told her where to find it." Her father's voice was growing weaker, blood loss likely taking his strength. She hated seeing him in this situation, suffering at the gunman's hand, but she appreciated his effort to distract the shooter from learning she was there.

A noise sounded from across the field. She listened. Heard a horse trotting. *Gavin?* Or was it just wishful thinking?

The gunman spun. "So, you were meeting someone, after all. No worries. I'll be long gone by the time the horse reaches us."

He shoved his hand into his pocket and came out holding a cell phone. He pressed his thumb to it, the phone coming alive and illuminating his face shield. She squinted to get a better look at his face, but the light reflected against the shield.

"I'm assuming you have another copy of these documents on the plane. Well, buh-bye, plane." He tapped his phone.

The plane erupted in a ball of fire. The ground beneath her feet rumbled in concussive waves. Fragments of the plane flew through the air and hit the dusty ground. A rush of heat washed over her face even at this distance.

She stared in stunned disbelief. Just who was this guy and how was he involved with her father?

"See how much you underestimated me," he shouted. "And don't think I believe you when you say you didn't give this information to your daughter. I won't rest until I'm sure she doesn't have it. Even if that means she has to die, too." He laughed, the sound high and maniacal, his craziness sending her fear skyrocketing.

He was willing to kill her father, so what would he do if he spotted her?

Horse hooves thundered on the open field.

Please let it be Gavin. As a former local deputy and now an FBI agent in Houston, he'd be armed and know what to do—how to save them.

Are You there, God? Listening? Please don't let this psycho fire on him, too.

The shooter mounted the bike. Kicked the engine awake then screeched to a start and roared forward, stopping to take a final shot at her father. The gun report sounded like thunder.

No. Oh, please, no. Had he done the unthinkable and killed her father?

Her head swam. Her leg muscles turned to mush. She grabbed the wall to keep from dropping to the ground.

Breathe deep. Keep it together.

The biker laughed again then shifted his bike into high speed, passing right in front of her. She held her breath so even the tiniest movement didn't give her away. The whoosh of wind from the cycle blasted her face and heavy fumes irritated her nose. He glanced her way. The gun lifting.

Had he seen her? She couldn't be sure and remained frozen in place.

When he moved out of sight, she ran for her dad. Knelt beside him. Spotted gaping chest and stomach wounds.

For a moment, all of her medical training and experience as a trauma nurse fled and panic won out. Her pulse skyrocketed. She felt woozy. Like she might collapse. She wanted to give in. To forget her father lay in front of her with wounds only a skilled surgeon could treat.

"Dad... I..." She didn't know how to continue as blood oozed from his body. If she'd listened to the many times he'd nagged her about becoming a doctor, she could help, but with his extensive injuries, only a doctor could save him now.

He moaned.

She let her gaze flick over the area. Searching for what, she didn't know. Maybe she was just avoiding the obvious.

Cut it out. He needs you to be strong. To think. Get it together.

She ripped off her favorite Christmas scarf, wadded it into a ball and pressed it against the most critical wound. Blood saturated the cashmere in moments and she suspected an equal amount of blood spurted from his back, too.

Please, she begged. *Don't let him die.*

"Lexie," he muttered, his voice not more than a whisper.

"Shh." She bent forward. "Don't try to talk."

He struggled to breathe, his chest barely moving. "Be

careful…dangerous. He took it. Your insurance. I should have…couldn't…my reputation. Legacy. He'll come after you, Lexie. He'll kill you…"

Gunshots. Lexie.

Gavin McKade cleared the tree line to see a fireball rising into the sky over an airplane torn in pieces and a dirt bike racing away from the maintenance shed.

Had Lexie given up on him because he was late and boarded the plane to go somewhere? Or were the gunshots directed at her and she'd been shot?

Dear God, don't let me be too late. Don't let Lexie be on that plane.

He jerked his unruly stallion's reins to keep him from bolting and searched for any sign of Lexie. He would call out, but with shots fired, he wasn't about to draw more attention to himself than Lightning's pummeling hooves might have already done.

Was she by the shed or in the plane?

He'd check the plane first. He kicked Lightning into motion. They tore across the open field, the biting wind hitting him full-on and carrying heavy black smoke in his direction. The heat soon forced him to pull up.

Dancing flames illuminated fragments of the plane lying scattered around. No one could have survived the fiery explosion. If she was in there— No, he wouldn't go there. Not until he checked by the shed.

He whipped Lightning around and took off. Nearing the shed, he spotted someone on the ground. Someone moving. Small. Slight. A woman. Leaning over another person. Performing CPR.

He threw caution to the wind and shouted, "Lexie!"

"Gavin!" she screamed. "Hurry."

Thank You, God, he prayed, though he had no idea if

God heard him. After shooting Emily, Gavin had been hard-pressed to trust in his faith.

Gavin pushed Lightning into a gallop, the stallion's breath coming in hard puffs as he quickly closed the distance between them. To be safe, he drew his weapon as he dismounted.

"Lexie," he said, afraid he was wrong, that she'd turn, it wouldn't be her, and he'd learn she'd perished in the explosion.

She looked up from doing CPR on a man.

It *was* Lexie. His Lexie. No…not his. Not anymore. He let out a slow breath of relief. "Are you okay?"

She stopped her compressions, held up blood-covered hands and peered down at the man lying in front of her.

"It's Dad. He…he's gone." A sob tore from her throat. "Gunshot wounds. I saw it all. He tried to give me an envelope and the guy shot him twice. Then took off. I tried to help Dad and failed."

"Oh, sugar, I'm so sorry." Gavin didn't think of the years that had passed…of the turmoil when they'd broken up. Instead, acting on pure instinct, he dropped down beside her and drew her into his arms. She snuggled tight against him, and he cradled her head against his chest as her body heaved with pain-filled sobs.

She needed his comfort, and he was only too happy to hold her, but with the shooting, he had to keep his gaze roving the area, just in case the killer hadn't really taken off.

He gently pushed back and gazed at her. "You said the shooter was gone."

"He took off on a dirt bike."

That explained the bike he'd seen.

"This can't be happening. Not really. Can it?" She suddenly grabbed Gavin's arm. "The killer can't get away with this. We have to go after him."

"He's long gone by now and we won't catch him on horseback." Gavin dug out his phone. "But I'll call Dad to get an alert out on the bike. Can you describe it?"

"Black, I think, but I'm not positive. Dark colored, anyway."

"Did it have a license plate?"

"I don't know. I was too afraid. I'm sorry." She wiped away her tears. "But the rider wore a leather jacket and pants. He was over six feet. Thin."

Without a better description of the bike, the odds were bad that they'd find the guy. Especially when a dirt bike could travel off-road.

"And the plane exploding?" Gavin asked. "Did the shooter have something to do with that, too?"

She nodded. "He used his phone to detonate it. Thank goodness Dad was flying his own plane and was alone."

"I'll want more details, but first I'll get that alert issued." Gavin dialed his father, Lake County sheriff Walt McKade, but stepped away from Lexie so he could speak freely about her father. He also didn't want her to learn that conversations with his dad were still tension-filled. No sense in adding to her stress.

As his phone rang, he kept her in view while also watching for any signs the shooter might have returned.

"Sheriff McKade," Gavin's dad answered with his usual confidence.

Just hearing his father's voice made him cringe, but he swallowed down his unease. "It's Gavin. There's been an explosion and shooting at the old airstrip on Engles ranch."

"I know about the explosion. Just got a 9-1-1 call from neighbors…but how do you know about it?"

"I'm in town for a few days."

"First I'm hearing about it," he grumbled. "And you just happened to be out at the airstrip when all of this goes down?"

"I'll explain that later," Gavin said. "For now, you need to know Dr. Grant's been fatally shot."

"Well, I'll be." His words were slow and drawn out in his thick drawl. "Here we all thought he was dead and now he turns up only to be murdered."

"Lexie's here, and she saw the whole thing. The shooter took off. Heading east on a dirt bike. She thinks it's black but she's not positive. He's been gone about five minutes or so. I thought you'd like to issue an alert ASAP."

"You got that right. I'll take care of it and head out there to get started on the investigation."

Great. The moment his dad arrived, he would demand to know Gavin's reasons for being in town.

He didn't have the authority to divulge that, yesterday, Dr. Grant had become a person of interest in a major health-care fraud investigation, and that Gavin had arrived to try to track him down.

"And before you try to claim jurisdiction on the murder…" his dad continued. "You know the ball's in my court, not you Feds."

Gavin stifled a groan. As far as he knew, his dad's only experience with the FBI was watching TV shows and movies that often got things wrong. Murder investigations didn't top the Bureau's priorities, and the Feds rarely involved themselves in a case without being invited.

"No worries there," Gavin said.

"I'll be there in less than ten." His dad disconnected the call.

Gavin returned to Lexie, who hadn't moved, her gaze fixed on her father. Gavin squatted next to her and told her softly, "Dad's on his way."

She sighed. "I suppose now would be a good time for you to tell me why you wanted to see me."

Though it was no longer necessary to locate her father, Gavin would still need to interview her and serve the warrant to search her father's office and home. Obviously, there was no point in the FBI filing charges against a deceased person, but his records could contain information about other doctors involved in the fraud. Still, nothing needed to be done tonight, and he'd hold off on upsetting her until after she'd gotten some rest.

"That can wait," he said.

She shook her head in wide sorrowful arcs. "You sound like my father. You both had these big things you needed to talk to me about. Turns out, he only wanted to give me that envelope. He tried, but it was so weird."

"Weird in what way?"

"He was acting totally out of character. All jittery and afraid. Clearly, he had a right to be. The shooter was creepy and not at all concerned about committing murder." She blew out an unsteady breath. "He said this would be his third strike, and he wasn't going back to prison. He also took the envelope and said he'd killed Dad's attorney in Mexico because Dad gave him the same information."

So Dr. Grant had been hiding out in Mexico this last month. But why? "Did the shooter mention what the envelope contained?"

She shook her head. "He did say he was part of some syndicate. Said Dad was meeting with the head honcho today, and the killer wasn't going to let that happen."

Gavin nodded but didn't speak. Dr. Grant wasn't the

only doctor in the fraud investigation. Gavin hadn't yet found a connection between the doctors, but he supposed it was possible they could have formed a syndicate and this murder was related.

"And there's more," she said. "The killer knew my name. Called me Dad's *precious Lexie*. Which means he didn't know Dad very well as I wasn't precious to him. Maybe once. When Mom was alive."

Gavin had hoped she'd reconciled with her father in the past few years, but clearly she'd still had issues with him. And now, thanks to her father, a killer knew her name.

Gavin didn't like it. Not one bit. He didn't want the killer to know anything about her. "In what context did he mention you?"

"He asked if Dad gave me the information, too. Dad said no, but the killer didn't believe him. Dad warned me before he died that this guy is dangerous, and he'll come after me. Kill me, too."

"Kill you?" Gavin's voice shot up, spooking Lexie and Lightning. He lowered his voice. "Do you have the information he's worried about?"

"I don't know what was in that envelope and Dad didn't give me anything else. But now that we know someone is looking for information, it makes sense that his office and house were ransacked." She turned her big-eyed gaze to him. "What if the killer spotted me as he was leaving? If he did, he knows I saw him commit murder." She shuddered. "Do you think he'll come after me? Try to kill me, too?"

"I won't let that happen, sugar. I promise." Gavin

wrapped an arm around her shoulders to help allay her fear, but his emotions were a different story.

If this man had killed once, he wouldn't hesitate to do so again, and now he had Lexie in his sights.

TWO

Lexie didn't know what to think. To feel. After Gavin's father arrived, he'd escorted her to the main road where she now sat sideways in the front of Sheriff McKade's patrol car, her feet planted on the asphalt as she waited to give her statement. She caught a glimpse in the distance of tall lights, their halos standing like beacons in the night over the plane wreckage, another set near her father's body, warning all who came close of the horrific sight.

And it had been horrific. There was no question. Even for a trauma nurse. Seeing the once-solid plane in tiny bits scattered around the area. Seeing her father gunned down. Worse than horrific.

She shuddered and stared at her blood-caked hands. Her father's blood. He'd lain in front of her, his life floating away, his eyes going blank and glazed. She'd seen death before. Of course she had. Many times in the ER. Always feeling sad for a life lost coupled with a bit of second-guessing as she ran the trauma through her brain to make sure they'd handled it right.

But tonight? What did she feel now?

Something, that was for sure, but it was hard to put a finger on her emotions. She definitely didn't feel the deep, split-your-insides-open anguish she'd experienced when her mother had died. So was it guilt for not being able to save her dad? Maybe. Actually, now that she took the time to think about it, she felt numb. Cold inside and out. Alone. So alone.

Where are You again, God? Why take someone else from my life? From Adam's life? Am I this undeserving of love?

Why was she even asking at this point in life? Nothing changed.

She wrapped her arms around her body and ran her hands up and down her arms to ward off the howling wind. Earlier, she'd tried closing the car door, but claustrophobia had set in and she'd had to open it again.

The sound of boots stomping across the road brought her head up in time to catch Sheriff McKade marching over to Gavin.

Gavin. What did she do about him? She'd been relieved to see him when he'd arrived. Practically thrown herself into his arms. But now what? Was *he* the reason for her numbness?

She shifted to get a better look at the pair. They stood strong, staring across the road, backs to her with hands on their waists in identical stances. They were both over six feet. Both had a head of thick, black hair, though she knew gray strands that had grown in numbers over the years intricately laced the sheriff's.

Gavin suddenly crossed his arms and spun. His dark gaze landed on her and that familiar, angry frustration with his dad lingered in his eyes. Walt turned, as well. They spit a few more sentences at each other and Gavin suddenly stormed in her direction.

Lexie sighed. Nothing had changed. The same old Gavin, and the same reason he'd left town. Left *her*.

Gavin was the firstborn in a family of four siblings,

and his father held his son to lofty standards that no one could live up to. Still, Gavin had wanted a career in law enforcement and the only option without leaving Lost Creek was to work as a deputy for his dad. He'd tried to make a go as a deputy for years. Really tried. Even if it meant he wasn't always happy.

Then one day he'd disagreed with direct orders from his father on how to handle a domestic disturbance. Walt had wanted to sit back and wait for things to play out. Not Gavin. He was more of a "take action and sort things out later" kind of guy. Fearing for the wife's safety, he'd stepped in. Tensions escalated and he'd ended up in a shoot-out with the husband, catching his wife in the cross fire. Emily had survived, and Gavin wasn't hurt, but from that day on, his father no longer trusted him.

No matter how hard Gavin worked to right things between them, he failed and couldn't continue to work with his father. His only choice was to leave town. At least, that was what he'd thought. Lexie still didn't agree.

Didn't matter now, though. She'd had enough of her pity party and it was time to shake it off. To go on. For Adam. Her brother needed her.

Gavin continued toward her, his strides long and powerful, his gaze focused.

Why was he in town, anyway? If it was solely to talk to her, why wouldn't he just tell her what he wanted to discuss? Why the big mystery?

Gavin stopped before her and squatted down.

How many times had she gazed into Gavin's rich brown eyes and known he was the man she'd wanted to marry? He'd dashed that dream when he'd moved away and left her behind without a second thought.

"Dad will take your statement," he finally said. "I was hoping to put it off till tomorrow, but he refused. So I wanted to see if you needed anything, and I'll take care of it while he's talking to you."

For a moment, he worked the muscles in his jaw then forced a smile. The left side tipped up just a fraction higher, a quirk that never failed to make Lexie's heart skip a beat.

"I could get some water for you," he offered. "A blanket. Or maybe I could call your aunt Ruth."

"Ruth? No. She's on a much-needed vacation, and I don't want to burden her with this until she gets back in a few days. But I do need to tell Adam about Dad." Lexie saw Walt approaching. "I'll give my statement to your dad and get going."

Gavin crossed his arms and gave her a steely look. "You're not going anywhere alone until this killer is caught."

"So you really *do* think he'll be coming after me," she said, letting her fear usurp her unease over his sudden bossiness.

"Yes," he said, but his narrowed gaze told her that he didn't like admitting it. "I'll drive you home, and make sure you have a protective detail. I can help you tell Adam, too."

No way she wanted Gavin to talk to Adam. The two of them had formed a strong bond and Gavin had destroyed the kid when he'd moved away. She'd have to tell Adam he'd lost his father. Why add the unease of talking to Gavin?

"I'm glad for the protection," she said. "But I'll deal with Adam on my own."

Walt arrived before them and slapped his hat on his head as he peered at Gavin. "Our first priority is to keep little Lexie safe. Since Ruth is in Florida, I planned to bring Lexie back to the ranch when I finish up here. I'll send a deputy to get Adam, too."

Lexie disliked it when he called her "little Lexie" and when he talked about her as if she was a child. It came across as demeaning, even though she knew he didn't mean it that way. He was just referring to her barely over five-foot height compared to his children, most of them six feet or more.

"I'm not letting Lexie out of my sight until I'm sure she has a strong detail assigned to her care," Gavin said. "Not with the threat the shooter made—and we have no way of knowing if he saw her. If he did, well…"

His worried tone sent her heart beating faster. "Do you think Adam could be in danger, too?"

"I suppose it's possible," Gavin said. "But I wouldn't expect your father to confide obviously valuable information to a kid. There'd be no point. If I was the killer, I'd focus on you, and then if I struck out, I'd move on to Adam."

"I concur," Walt added. "Especially since your dad has never even lived with Adam and isn't much involved in his life."

They both made valid points. Her father had blamed Adam for the loss of the love of his life. Not a legitimate blame, but her dad had associated Adam with the pain and never bonded with him. He'd also claimed Lexie resembled her mother and had hardly been able to look at her. He'd promptly moved her and Adam into Aunt Ruth's house, where they'd both lived for the last fourteen years. So when Lexie's heart was shattered by the loss of her mother, she'd lost her father, too. Now she'd lost him for good. Tears threatened again, but she firmed her resolve to keep it together until she was alone.

"Still, we'll take no chances, and we'll watch over

Adam, too." Gavin lifted his chin as if daring his father to disagree.

"That we will." The sheriff kept his gaze leveled on Lexie. "So what'll it be, sweetheart? Gavin drives you home or you come to the ranch?"

Even with the simmering tension between her and Gavin, being at Trails End Ranch with this strong law-enforcement family was a safe place while she thought through the implications of all that had happened tonight. Besides, she missed his mother, Winnie, and his grandparents, Jed and Betty. Jed would offer to protect her and both of the women would fuss over her, and right now, she could use a little comfort along with the added protection.

"I rode Misty over here, and I need to get her home and brushed down."

"You can do that at the ranch. 'Sides, Tessa and Kendall would let me have an earful if I didn't bring you home. I won't even put voice to what Winnie would do to me." At the mention of his daughters and wife, a slow smile slid across Walt's lips.

"Tessa and Kendall are both at the ranch?" Gavin asked.

"Not just yet. But seein's how you're in town for once, I figured we should get the whole family together, so I called them."

"I don't think Lexie wants to get into the middle of all of that." Gavin puffed out his chest, his white dress shirt straining at the buttons.

Irritation shot through her. He'd not only gotten bossy, but he also seemed to think he could make her decisions for her when he had no right.

"I'll be glad to come to the ranch," she said, ignoring Gavin's disappointed look. "But I want to be sure no one tells Adam about Dad. I want to do it."

"Matt's on duty," Walt said, mentioning Gavin's younger brother. "I'll assign him to pick Adam up. Matt'll keep it on the down low if I tell him to."

Gavin took a sharp intake of air through his nose, his nostrils flaring. He couldn't have missed his dad's less-than-subtle message that at least one son listened to him.

Gavin turned to Lexie. "I'll round up our horses and we can ride over together."

"Little late to be riding, isn't it?" Walt asked.

"We both got here just fine on horseback. We can get home the same way." Gavin eyed his father for a moment as if challenging him to argue.

Instead, Walt faced Lexie.

Gavin strode off into the dark.

"Stubborn boy," Walt muttered.

"Gavin's thirty-five. Not much of a boy anymore."

Walt scowled at her and pulled a small notebook from his uniform pocket. "I'm guessing you have a horse trailer nearby as you sure as shootin' didn't ride cross-county on your horse."

"My truck and trailer are down by the cutoff at Wheeler's old gas station."

"Then I'll make sure someone escorts you back there at the end of the night and helps you load your horse."

One of the things she liked about Walt McKade was that, behind all his bluster and bravado, he had a compassionate side. Despite being ornery at times and tough on his kids, he was a gentleman through and through, and he'd raised his sons to be fine, responsible men.

"I'm sorry about your father, Lexie," he said, his words filled with earnest compassion.

The soft tone coming from such a tough lawman made it even harder to keep tears in check, but Lexie managed it.

"Thank you," she said.

He stroked his salt-and-pepper mustache for a moment as if trying to decide how to move forward. "S'posin you give me the details of what happened tonight."

She replayed the night, making sure to include every point she could remember, and he recorded them in his notebook.

"Did you know before today that your daddy was back in town?" His pen hovered over the page.

"No. He called after dinner, and that's the soonest I heard about it."

"And he came back just to give you the envelope that was stolen?"

She shrugged. "The plane was on the ground when I got here, so I don't know how long he'd been here. He did say he had another appointment, so who knows how many people he talked to before me, or would have after, if he'd lived." A lump rose to her throat but she swallowed hard. "The shooter mentioned that Dad was going to meet the head of a syndicate."

"Syndicate, huh?" Walt made a production of closing his notebook and stowing it with his pen, then tipping his hat back even farther and leaning on the car door. "A syndicate doesn't on the surface suggest illegal activities, and I'm not at all saying your daddy was involved in something illegal, but being killed in relationship to it is a whole other ball game."

She'd been thinking the same thing—that was, when she could forget the horror of seeing him gunned down and think clearly at all. "All I know is it's not normal for a man to disappear for a month, and when he does resurface, he's killed."

"Agreed. Matt's already working on tracking down

the biker." He pursed his lips. "We've secured the area and I've called in the ATF to investigate the explosion."

"ATF?" Lexie asked.

"Bureau of Alcohol, Tobacco, Firearms and Explosives. They investigate bombs and have resources we don't begin to possess and can pinpoint the type of explosion."

"How will that help find Dad's killer?"

"Forensic evidence from the bomb could lead us to where the suspect purchased or stole his supplies. Finding that could then lead us to the suspect."

"And what will your role be?"

"My team will work the murder angle and try to locate this syndicate you mentioned. Since we've already tried to find a lead as to your father's disappearance this past month and failed, I'm not sure how successful we'll be, but I aim to try." He shifted his duty belt. "I'll also come up with a plan to make sure you stay safe, sweetheart."

"I'd appreciate that." Her gaze drifted to Gavin, who was standing by the horses, his phone to his ear. She couldn't help but wish he would stay in town and hunt down this killer. Despite their differences, with his FBI experience, she'd feel safest if he was the one to protect her.

How crazy was that? He'd walked out on her—left her heart shattered—and here she was, wanting him to protect her. Or was she simply fooling herself? Trying to believe she needed him to keep her safe when in reality she was simply happy to see him again?

Gavin kept Lexie in view as he waited for his supervisor to call back. She still sat in the squad car, but his dad had stepped away. The dome light caught the golden strands of her hair, wavy to her shoulders. Her icy-blue eyes, dark with angst, stared across the field, her arms wrapped around a slender waist. She'd always been a beautiful woman, but it was all he could do not to stare at her and let her know how much simply looking at her impacted him.

Was she thinking about her father or about their past? He suspected both. Man, he wanted to help her through this, but that was the last thing she would want. He'd hurt her in the worst possible way. He'd acted just like her father and put her second in his life.

He hadn't meant for things to end between them, least of all to end so badly. Just like he hadn't meant to shoot Emily, but he had, and she now had a permanent limp thanks to him.

His phone rang. Assistant Special Agent in Charge Zachary Harrison's name flashed on the screen. Gavin quickly answered the call, but took a breath to make sure he displayed the confidence needed for lead agent on the investigation. His first lead. Exactly what he'd planned when he'd taken a series of online business classes so he could be assigned to the white-collar crimes unit, a division with great potential for advancement. Sure, Harrison had made Gavin lead agent on this investigation because of his connection to Lost Creek, but he still felt the need to prove himself.

He quickly and succinctly explained the latest developments with Dr. Grant. "A syndicate could mean the doctors on our list are connected."

"I concur," Harrison replied.

"I want to remain in Lost Creek and work with County on the murder investigation. I have the feeling it ties in with the other doctors involved in the Medicaid scam."

"You could be right," Harrison said. "Your connections could very well pay off for us. Making you lead might just be the smartest move I've made all week."

"If you remember, my dad and I don't see eye to eye on investigative protocols, so my working with him isn't as certain as you think."

"Still, he's your father and, from what you've told me, he's a good sheriff. He'd be a fool to reject our help."

"Did I mention he's stubborn?"

"Then the apple doesn't fall far from the tree." Harrison chuckled.

Gavin wouldn't discuss the point further. One way or another he'd find a way to get his dad on his side. Since the job was all he had in his life right now, it was imperative that he advance, and that wouldn't happen if he failed on this investigation. "I'll need to fill in my dad and his investigator on the Medicaid case."

"Go ahead. Who knows? Maybe working a joint investigation with your father is just the thing you need to learn how to let go of controlling every little thing around you. It could even improve your teamwork."

In Gavin's last evaluation, his skills and abilities received high marks. But being a team player? Not so much. His fault totally. He compensated for shooting Emily by controlling everything and didn't trust others. If he ever hoped to advance, he needed to change. He'd known it for some time, but hadn't found a way to do so.

"Anything else?" Harrison asked.

"With Dr. Graves's death, I think his daughter would be more apt to cooperate if I share her father's suspected Medicaid fraud."

"Keep the information superficial, and I'm okay with that."

Gavin agreed and ended the call by promising to keep Harrison apprised of the situation.

He stowed his phone then grabbed Misty and Lightning's reins and led the pair across the field.

Lexie flipped up her faux-fur-trimmed hood and started toward him. She wore the same worn red cowboy boots she'd owned for years. Man, he'd loved to tease her about those boots. Her feet were tiny, and she'd had to buy them in the children's department. Despite the circumstances, he smiled.

She took Misty's reins. "Looks like you think something's funny."

"Your boots."

She shot him a look, but frustration quickly melted into an impish smile that never failed to tug at his heart. "I know you like to make fun of them, but you wouldn't laugh so hard if you knew how much less I pay for my boots than the rest of you do. Besides, I look far less comical in my boots than you do getting ready to mount a horse in your city-slicker pants and shiny shoes."

Gavin grimaced. Right…his shoes. He'd planned to talk to her, take Lightning back to the ranch for a quick brush-down then head for his motel for the night before he ran into his father. Now here he was, looking out of place with all his old wounds raw and on display for Lexie. She'd seen enough of his ongoing issues with his father over the years. Something he wasn't proud of. He was a grown man. Old enough to be a father himself, for crying out loud. He sure should be old enough not to let his father continue to push his buttons. Not something he could change standing here.

"We should get going," he said. "Let me give you a leg up."

Her eyes narrowed for a moment but then she nodded. Misty was getting on in years, so he suspected her agreement was for the mare's well-being, as a shorter person mounting a horse from the ground was hard on the horse.

Gavin hoisted her into the saddle then climbed on Lightning. His shoe slipped in the stirrup and he regretted being so hasty in not changing his attire. He'd regretted it even more when his father eyed his shoes and chuckled.

Lexie set Misty in motion and he directed Lightning to move into position beside her. He kept his head on a swivel, carefully watching the trees dipping in the wind.

Maybe his behavior was overkill, but he'd learned the hard way that things could go sideways in a hurry. He wasn't about to make the same mistake again. Not with Lexie's life in the balance.

THREE

Gavin led Lexie under the wood sign stretching over Trails End's driveway. His ancestors had burned the ranch name and MK brand into the wood that had been erected in 1895 when the ranch was first established. About the time the first McKade had become county sheriff. With minor repairs, it had stood the test of time and always gave Gavin a sense of pride in his family's long history.

They trotted down the familiar drive until the two-story home with a long porch holding strings of garland and colorful Christmas lights came into view. Lights glowed from the lower windows, which meant his family was gathered in the living and dining rooms that faced the front of the house. A patrol car sat at the end of a circular drive—Matt's car, Gavin presumed.

He veered off shy of the house and dismounted at the corral abutting a large barn and stable. "We'll leave the horses here. I'll make sure someone takes care of them."

Gavin thought to help Lexie dismount, but he knew she'd balk, so he secured the reins and they made their way up an incline to the house. They'd barely stepped onto the porch when the door flew open and his mother barreled out like a bronc in a rodeo shoot. She was thin and tall, with leathery skin from time spent outdoors, and had a solid look about her as if she'd sunk her roots into the ground like the mighty cypress trees in the area. She'd always worked the ranch with the hands and kids, and never taken a day off.

"Welcome home, son." Her arms outstretched, she jerked him to her as if he was a rag doll, and he went willingly.

After getting her fill, she set him away and stepped to Lexie. "You poor dear. Come here."

His mother's strong arms swallowed Lexie and she started to cry.

Gavin's heart ached, and he felt like a dolt standing there when he knew if he hadn't moved to Houston, she would be crying on his shoulder, not his mom's. But he didn't have long to dwell on it as his grandmother burst through the door and made a beeline toward him. She wore a gingham top over a T-shirt, and when she pulled him close, she was soft and squishy and smelled of baking spices. She did all the cooking, and he'd never found a better meal than the hearty ones she served up.

"Nana." He hugged her back.

A clap on his shoulder had him pulling back to look into the sharp blue eyes of his granddad's lined face. "About time you got here. S'posin your daddy kept you sitting around all this time."

"Crime scenes take time to process." Gavin was surprised he was defending his father.

His granddad hooked his thumbs in his red suspenders. "In my day, we wouldn't make a little bit of a thing like Lexie wait around. We'd drive her home and have a civil conversation over a cup of coffee."

"Coffee sounds like a good idea." Gavin's mother took Lexie's arm. "We'll settle you and Adam in the dining room by yourselves, and the two of you can take as long as you want."

"Dad will likely have additional questions for Lexie when he gets here," Gavin said.

"Then he'll just have to wait." His mother's jaw firmed, meaning his dad would indeed be kept waiting, as Winnie McKade was the only person with the power to make that happen.

"I'll see to the horses," Granddad said.

"I appreciate that."

"Don't worry so much, Grandson," Nana murmured. "God is faithful and He will work all of this for Lexie's good."

If only Gavin could be certain about that, but he hadn't been certain about anything since Emily had been shot other than needing to leave town. He followed his family into the wide foyer holding a towering Christmas tree filled with handmade ornaments dating back as far as his granddad's childhood.

Lexie glanced back at Gavin and, if he didn't know better, he'd think she was begging him to join her to help break the news to Adam. But Gavin *did* know better. She didn't want his help. She'd made that perfectly clear. Besides, he'd given up the right to sit by her side in good times and bad, and no matter how much he hated seeing her pain, he wasn't a comfort to her now.

He closed the door behind them and headed across the house's original wide-plank floors. Through a wide archway, he saw the other family members settle in front of a roaring fire, the woodsy campfire aroma he loved mingling with the scent of pine.

Matt stepped out to meet Gavin in the foyer. Though an investigator, Matt still worked patrol when needed and was dressed in the department's basic navy patrol uniform. He looked tired and concerned, but had a ready smile.

He gave a light punch to Gavin's arm. "You sure do know how to make an entrance in town, bro."

"I'm surprised to see you here. I'd have thought you'd be out investigating the murder."

"You know Dad. He has to make sure the department is fairly represented. So he'll be in the thick of this one to make sure we don't garner any bad press." Matt frowned, disturbing his pretty-boy face that assured he always had his share of women to date. "And if you must know, I *am* involved. I've been tracking the suspect's dirt bike."

"Any luck with that?" Gavin asked.

"You know Dad wouldn't want me to share investigative details outside the department." A single eyebrow arched, looking so like their dad's mannerism.

Gavin had to work hard not to comment. "And I also know you're going to tell me everything, so why hassle me in the process?"

"I am, am I?"

Truth be told, Gavin wasn't as confident as he'd once been that Matt would spill the beans. His brother had grown up a lot in the last few years. He'd be making a run for sheriff when their dad retired, and Gavin honestly believed Matt, who'd just turned thirty-one, could handle the position.

"Okay, fine," his brother said without further prodding. "There's no harm in telling you that ATF investigators arrived on scene and have taken over. They shooed Tessa away and I hear tell she's hopping mad."

"She had to know it was coming." Gavin imagined their youngest sibling, who was a sworn deputy along with being a top forensic crime scene investigator for the county, facing off with an ATF agent. She was a nurturer at heart, but let anyone threaten her work domain, and she turned into a tiger.

"Knowing is one thing. Having a Fed toss you off the scene in your own county is another."

"Hey, now. It's awfully soon in my homecoming to be bashing the Feds, isn't it?"

Matt frowned. "Dad said you wouldn't tell him why you were in town."

"I'm here on an investigation that involves Dr. Grant."

"For real?"

Gavin nodded. "I cleared it with my supervisor to fill you and Dad in, but you'll have to wait until I get Lexie settled and make sure we've made a protection plan for her and Adam."

"Then in the spirit of cooperation, I can tell you that I located the dirt bike abandoned a few miles from the airfield."

He narrowed his eyes. "How can you be so sure it's the right bike?"

"The envelope with Lexie's name on it was in a saddle-bag. Empty, of course."

"She told me the shooter has been incarcerated before. So any prints Tessa lifts should return an ID in the database."

"Don't hold your breath, bro. Lexie also told Dad that the suspect wore gloves. I doubt we'll get prints."

"What about the bike's registration?"

"Bike's not street legal, so no plates, but Kendall's looking up the VIN number as we speak." Their other sister, Kendall, had worked part-time as a deputy for nine years while she'd worked on her degree in information technology and was now a full-time deputy.

"Okay, so say this *is* the bike ridden by our suspect,"

Gavin said. "No way if he owns the bike that he would abandon it and let us run the title to discover his identity."

"So it's likely stolen, but we haven't had any dirt bikes reported stolen." Matt frowned. "We'll just have to wait on Kendall."

Gavin didn't want to wait. He'd rather log in to the database and get an instant answer. But taking over someone's work was the kind of thing that drove others crazy. He would hold off for a bit, but if they didn't hear from his sister soon, he would take charge and deal with the consequences later. "People around here don't always register new bikes. It could also be secondhand and not registered to begin with."

"Then if the VIN leads nowhere, we'll need another way to find the owner." Matt hooked his thumbs in the corner of his pants' pockets.

His brother might be taking the wait-and-see approach, but Gavin wasn't about to take the laid-back approach. "We need to figure it out ASAP so we're ready to act if needed."

"Whoa. When did you become such an all-fire control freak?" Matt shook his head. "City living, I suppose, but you're back home now. You'll need to learn to relax again or you'll tick people off."

Gavin wouldn't admit the incident with his dad had changed him. Better to let Matt blame it on the city and move on. "You're running the envelope for DNA, too, right?"

Matt crossed his arms. "We may not be a big, fancy department, but we do know how to investigate a crime."

"I didn't mean it that way, and you know it."

Matt continued to eye him.

"I'm gonna grab a cup of coffee. You want one?"

Gavin asked before saying something else to make his brother mad.

"Yeah, sure."

Gavin led the way to the kitchen. He glanced through the dining room's French doors to see Lexie with her arm wrapped around Adam's shoulders. Dark pain lingered in her eyes and cut Gavin to the quick. Adam, the teenager Gavin had come to care for, darted his gaze around the room, as if looking for a way to flee or for help in dealing with his grief.

Lexie met Gavin's gaze and frowned before looking away. He sighed. He hadn't meant to hurt her. He'd asked her to move to Houston with him, but her dad had forbidden her to move Adam out of town. Made no sense. Not when her father had little to do with either of them, but still, he'd had legal custody of Adam. Which meant she'd be stuck in Lost Creek for years. Gavin had suggested a long-distance relationship, but she'd shut him down fast.

Although a part of him wished he could go back and change things, he'd been right to move to Houston. Confirmed it, too, the minute he'd talked to his father tonight. But, no matter what, Gavin wasn't going to flake on her now. He wasn't going anywhere. At least not until he was confident she was safe.

FOUR

Lexie tightened her hold on Adam's hand, but he was trying so hard to be a grown-up that he shrugged free and jumped to his feet. He marched across the room and lifted a stuffed Santa Claus from an antique sideboard to stare at it.

"I know Dad has been a loser father," Adam said, "but I can't believe he'd get involved in something illegal."

"We don't know that he broke the law," she said, wishing the same comfort she'd once offered for skinned knees would work for Adam tonight. "Just that he was involved with a syndicate of some sort."

He spun around. "Sounds bad, though, right?"

She got up to join him but shoved her hands in her pockets to keep from reaching out to him. "That's because in our world the word 'syndicate' often refers to a group involved in illegal activities."

Adam's eyes, blue and large like their father's, narrowed. "Yeah. Dad getting shot makes it almost a certainty."

"Perhaps."

He set down the Santa and it toppled to the floor. He stared at it. "What do you think he was mixed up in?"

"I don't know."

"Had to be drugs." He grabbed the Santa Claus and settled it on the shelf with great force.

Due to his grief, she ignored the way he manhandled the keepsake item the McKades had owned for generations. "Why would you say drugs?"

"Dunno. Just sounds likely is all." He chewed on his lower lip. "Do you think I'm in danger, too?"

"I hope not." She played it down so she didn't terrify him more. "Either way, we both need to be extra careful. As of this minute, there'll be no going anywhere without me at your side."

An impish grin lit his face. "Cool. That means no school."

"You wish." She knuckled his head. "I can't have you fall behind."

"But I'll be alone."

"I'll see if Gavin or the sheriff can arrange to have someone go to school with you."

"Gavin. *Pfft.* Why's he even here?" Adam dropped onto the nearest chair, sliding down so far, she thought he'd slip off.

"I don't know, but he can help us, so we have to give him a chance." She couldn't believe she'd not only downplayed their father's actions, but now she was standing up for Gavin. What was next? Welcoming Gavin back into their lives?

No. No way.

"Like you're happy to see him," Adam muttered.

"I was when he came to my aid at the airstrip," she admitted and left it at that. The last thing either of them needed was to get into a heated discussion about Gavin. "Let me see if the sheriff arrived and we're cleared to go home."

"Home?" His voice squeaked. "Is it safe?"

Gone was his bravado. Sitting before her was the little boy she'd held during crazy Texas thunderstorms. Comforted after their beloved pets had died. When he'd gotten his immunizations…and on and on. Her anger flared. How could their father put them in this position? Easy. He thought only of himself.

She squeezed Adam's shoulder. "If Sheriff McKade or Gavin say it's not safe, we won't go there. Okay?"

"But where will we stay?"

"Let me talk to them and we'll figure something out."

She stepped out of the room, closing the door behind her. Walt had returned from the crime scene and he sat with Kendall on the old plaid sofa. Gavin and Matt both leaned against a wall as if they planned to spring into action. His mother and grandparents sat in side chairs, both ladies crocheting.

"Can I speak to you a minute, Sheriff?" Lexie called out as soon as there was a break in the conversation.

She felt Gavin's gaze on her, but she wouldn't make eye contact. His father got up and strode toward her, no questions asked. Gavin pushed off the wall and tagged along. Walt frowned at Gavin, but he held his ground as if he'd been standing up to his father all his life, when in fact all of the McKade siblings tried not to buck Walt's decisions unless it was of utmost importance.

"I told Adam about Dad," she said to them both. "But I didn't want to terrify him, so I didn't share details like Dad's warning. I'd appreciate it if you all kept it to yourselves, too."

"Makes sense," Gavin said. "But he needs to know the suspect is looking for something and will likely come back. And that he might have seen you, too."

"I made sure Adam understands enough to know he

needs to be careful. For the most part, he's trying to act tough, but I can tell he's afraid."

Walt offered a kind smile. "Nothing to worry about. Gavin here has insisted on personally seeing you home tonight."

Gavin nodded and met her gaze. "I just want to be sure you're safely settled in, is all."

"Thank you," she said instead of trying to argue when she was so wiped out.

"We've got a deputy stationed outside your house for the night," Walt continued. "Kendall will drive Adam to school in the morning and spend the day with him. After we have a clearer picture of what happened at the scene and have processed any recovered evidence, we'll make a long-term plan."

Her heart dropped. "Do you really think this will go long-term?"

Walt rubbed his forehead lined from hours of working the ranch beneath the hot Texas sun. "Can't rightly say. Not when I don't have enough information."

"Regardless, it's best to be prepared," Gavin said.

She firmed her jaw, something she often felt like her slight stature forced her to do to be taken seriously. "I'd like to be in on all discussions about our protection."

Walt nodded. "Let's plan to meet over lunch here tomorrow. If you have to go anywhere before then, our deputy will follow you. That work for you, sweetheart?"

At his tender tone, she almost lost it. Walt was a hard taskmaster with Gavin, but once she'd started dating Gavin, Walt had in many ways become the father she'd always wanted. Until Gavin had left. Then she'd made a point of trying not to run into any of the McKades if she could help it.

"Can we meet at one? Adam only has a half day tomorrow, so I'll need to pick him up from school early."

"Kendall can bring him home."

"I know, but I want to try to keep as much of our routine as possible to reduce his turmoil over losing Dad."

"I completely understand," Walt said. "Adam can have lunch in the kitchen with my parents while we talk. Mom will fill him up with her famous Christmas cookies."

Lexie smiled her thanks.

"Are you ready to go?" Gavin asked.

She nodded. "Let me get Adam."

She went to the dining room door and motioned for her brother to join her in the foyer. He started off at a good clip, his untied sneakers slapping on the floor, but then he spotted Gavin and slowed.

Gavin smiled. "Good to see you, bud."

"We're not buds." Adam jerked open the front door and bounded down the stairs.

"Hey, wait up!" Gavin went charging after Adam to grab his arm.

The teen shook it off.

"Look, I get that you're mad at me," Gavin said. "You have every right to be, but I need you to stick close by me or any deputies escorting you. For safety reasons. Can you do that?"

Adam nodded, but his sullen expression remained. "Let's just get going."

"My car is over there." Gavin gestured at his black SUV backed into a small parking area next to the house.

When they were on the road, Lexie glanced over the seat to where Adam glared at the back of Gavin's head.

How had their lives come to this? To the point that she and her little brother were in serious danger? Bad enough that she had to deal with it, but Adam was just a kid.

Adam slammed a fist on his knee and jerked his head toward the window. She caught a glimpse of pain mingling with anger in his eyes. He'd taken the news of their father's death harder than she'd expected, but part of the pain, and she suspected all of the anger, was her fault. Her breakup with Gavin had devastated Adam. He'd lost the male role model that he'd bonded with most. And now he had to deal with the emotions of losing a father who should have been that positive role model in the first place.

Lexie sighed. She would just have to limit Adam's exposure to Gavin to make things easier for him. Just like she needed to limit her own exposure.

Right. Easier said than done when her gaze kept drifting to him. Settling on his broad shoulders and strong jaw. His long, masculine fingers as he rested his hand on the gearshift. And then there was the scent of his woodsy cologne, now mixed with the smell of hay and horses. At their lunch meeting tomorrow, she'd make sure he understood that he didn't owe her anything and that if he wanted to go back to Houston, that was fine with her. But even as the thought popped into her head, she doubted it *was* okay.

"Grrr," she said without thinking.

Gavin glanced at her. "Everything okay?"

"It's nothing." A big, fat nothing that was everything to her at the moment. She followed Adam's lead and peered out the window, too.

The SUV rounded a narrow curve to where she'd parked her truck and trailer. Gavin pulled into the boarded-up gas station. The station had gone out of business when Mr. Engles had closed down his airstrip and barricaded access for vehicles beyond this point in an effort to keep out trespassers.

Gavin angled his vehicle to shine headlights on her truck before shifting into Park.

Exhausted, it took all her strength to push open the door and climb down, but she wouldn't let Adam or Gavin witness her fatigue. It was a good thing Gavin had such a considerate grandfather who'd bedded Misty down at the ranch for the night. Lexie loved her horse, but was glad not to have to take care of her on top of everything else.

Gavin headed straight for her truck. Why, she didn't know, but she didn't have the energy to question him. She opened the SUV's back door for Adam. He slid out, his shoulders sagging, his face downcast.

"I know this is hard." She forced out a smile. "But we'll get through it just like we get through everything else life throws at us. With our faith."

Right. Faith. She felt like a hypocrite. Hers had pretty much been put on the back burner since their mom died, but she didn't want to impact Adam's faith journey by letting him know she had doubts on God's faithfulness, so she put on a good front.

He gave her another sullen look and leaned against the SUV.

She stifled a sigh, something she'd been doing since he'd become a teenager and spread wings she'd had to clip at times. Aunt Ruth was a great mother figure, but Lexie felt pressure to fulfill her mother's dying wishes. She'd known their father could get wrapped up in his practice and forget everything else, so she'd asked Lexie to make sure Adam was happy and well looked after.

She'd kept that promise and wasn't about to let a killer or even Gavin's attention make her shirk her responsibilities. She dug out her keys and started for the truck. She heard Adam's shoes thumping on the concrete behind her.

Gavin approached the passenger door. He spun around, his gaze intense. "Back to the car. Both of you."

Lexie looked past him to see her truck window shattered and the door standing open.

Her heart racing, she grabbed Adam's arm and dragged him back to the SUV.

Gavin eased forward, his feet crunching over glass. She noted her truck's dome light was out, so the person who'd broken the window had either turned it off or shattered it, as well. Lexie still had her hand on Adam's arm, which shook under her grasp. Stepping closer to him, she slid her arm around his waist. He was nearly six feet tall now and she couldn't place an arm around his shoulders or she'd do so. He started to shrug her off, maybe thinking he needed to be that tough young man again, but then stopped and moved a bit closer.

Gavin drew out his phone and turned on the flashlight app while still balancing his gun. He crept quietly around the truck, shining the beam in the surrounding shrubs and dense foliage. Then he moved to the horse trailer hitched to the back of her truck and peered inside.

He faced them. "Looks like they're gone."

Adam let out a long sigh and pushed free of Lexie's hold.

Gavin holstered his weapon. "I'll take you home, then come back to handle the scene with Dad and Tessa."

"That's fine." Lexie shouldn't let him take over for her, but she didn't want Adam to stand around looking at the destruction. "I picked up a prescription at the pharmacy and need to grab it from the glove box."

"Is that really necessary tonight?"

She nodded, thinking he didn't need to know that the doctor had put Adam on ADD medication.

"Then I need to warn you. The inside of the truck

is trashed, and the medication could have been stolen."
Adam got in the SUV, and Gavin walked her to the truck.
He shone his light inside.

Lexie gasped and forgot all about the prescription. In
the bright beam, glass sparkled from the slashed-open
seats. The mats had been jerked out and the carpet torn
up. The glove box hung open and items she'd stored in
the jump seat were scattered across the floor and ground.

Gavin leaned in behind her, focusing his light in the
cab. She felt the heat of his body, but forgot even that
when the light landed on a piece of paper lying next to a
cell phone on the seat.

"That's not my phone." She reached for it.

"Don't touch it," Gavin warned. He focused the light
on the paper with its big bold letters and read the message.

"'I want the information. Give it to me before I have
to take more drastic actions. Keep this phone with you
at all times. I'll call with further instructions.'"

"The killer?" She spun to look at Gavin, finding him
even closer than she thought. She could easily imagine
his strong arms going around her right now, offering the
comfort he'd so often provided in the past. For that very
reason, she pushed him back. "The killer must have seen
me and didn't trust that Dad was telling the truth."

"So he thinks your dad gave you the information."

"But what could it be?"

Gavin met her gaze and held it. The dark worry she
saw in his eyes told her bad news was coming. "It likely
has to do with what I wanted to talk to you about. I came
back to town to investigate your father."

"You *what*?"

"I'd hoped to do a better job of telling you, but my

team has been investigating health-care fraud and your dad just came on our radar."

"No, I don't believe it." She shook her head hard. "Not Dad. He may not have been a great father, but he would never sink that low."

"I hoped the same thing, Lex, but we have to face facts now. Someone killed him. Someone who's part of a syndicate."

Gavin took her hand, but she couldn't think clearly with him touching her, so she jerked it free.

"It's looking more and more like he was involved with some unsavory people," Gavin continued, his tone deadly serious. "We need to figure out who they are and what they're looking for before they try to kill you, too."

FIVE

Gavin stood at the front door to Ruth Paulson's house, staring at its fragrant pine wreath and big red bow while Lexie worked the lock. As soon as she opened the door, Adam bolted inside and up the stairs.

"Thank you for driving us home." Lexie started to close the door.

He reached over her head to plant a hand on the door. "Before I go, I'd like to take a look around to make sure the place is secure."

"I'll agree on one condition." Her gaze locked on his.

"Name it."

"You steer clear of Adam," she said firmly. "He's had enough drama for tonight without having to deal with issues over your abandonment."

Another fist to his heart. He deserved this one, too. He sucked in a breath. Let it out. He had to find a way to forget their past and concentrate on the lives that could be lost if he let emotions make his decisions for him. "I'll have to check the locks on his window."

"Then I'll come with you and run interference. We'll start there so he can get some sleep." She hooked her jacket on the newel post and marched up the stairs.

At the landing, she tucked her plaid blouse into her

jeans and tugged on the thick belt boasting a silver buckle. She was a Texan to the core like most everyone who lived in rural Lake County. Something he'd forgotten since living in the city.

He followed her down the hallway and stepped into Adam's messy room to get to the window. The teen glared at Gavin, who cringed at the walls reverberating with the loud, blaring music coming from Adam's speakers. Gavin wasn't one to judge. He'd been the same as a teen. Man, that seemed like an eternity ago. Still, he wouldn't mind going back to those days when he and his dad were inseparable—his family everything to him.

Stop it. Focus.

Lexie chatted with Adam while Gavin checked the lock. Once finished, he wasted no time leaving the teen alone and then followed Lexie through all five bedrooms on the second floor and the first-floor rooms, tugging at windows and double-checking locks in the rooms with exterior doors. She didn't say a word through the tour, but the moment he finished, she marched to the front door and pulled it open. Clearly, she wanted him gone.

He had no excuse to stay, even more reason to go, but his feet were made of lead and he couldn't step through that door.

She turned to look at him, her gaze pointed.

"I know Ruth always has coffee on hand," he said, grasping for any reason not to leave. "How about I make a fresh pot and we talk?"

"About what?"

He winced at her suspicious tone, but wouldn't back down. "Your father."

She nipped on her lower lip and didn't move an inch. "I do want to know about your investigation, but you have to promise not to bring up anything personal. I'm too exhausted for that."

"I promise."

She led him into the kitchen and opened the back door. Two large German shepherds charged into the house and pawed her legs.

"Well, hello to you, too." She laughed and gave them both big kisses on their heads.

Feeling a bit jealous of the dogs, Gavin sat at the round oak table worn from years of family use. "Nice to see Salt and Pepper are still doing well."

Lexie dumped kibble into two large bowls. "They have the best vet around."

Ruth was a highly respected veterinarian, and she filled the ranch with a menagerie of animals needing homes. She brought many of them home while waiting for someone to adopt them, but they never ended up leaving.

Lexie washed her hands and prepared the coffee in a single-serve machine. He watched her every move. She wasn't what people would call an overly graceful woman. She could be, he supposed, if she didn't often rush head-on into things and stumble in her eagerness. Her father's extreme demands when she was young had taught her to hurry to please him. That was a subject the two of them had often commiserated about in the time they'd been a couple.

The nutty aroma of coffee drifted through the homey kitchen. When the first cup finished, he reached out to take it from her, but she made a point of setting it on the table as if making sure she avoided his touch. She then placed a milk jug and sugar bowl next to it.

"Thank you." The fact that she remembered how he took his coffee only added to his sadness over the end of their relationship. And the way she avoided touching him? Man, that hurt, too.

She went to retrieve the other cup and then sat across the table from him. He opened his mouth to ask how she was doing but then snapped it shut.

She met his gaze. "Go ahead and say it."

"Say what?"

"You forget… I know you like the back of my hand. You were going to say something then stopped."

"It's personal."

"Oh, okay. In that case, never mind." She crossed her arms as if defending herself against him.

He felt like such a jerk for adding to her pain. He wished things could be different, but he'd had to leave town or die a slow death working for his father.

She met his gaze. "So tell me about the investigation into my dad."

"First, you should know that I can only share the barest of details because you don't have clearance to be read in."

"Read in? Fancy talk for a guy from Lost Creek." She frowned. "What with your new way of dressing, I should have expected that, I guess."

"Now who's getting personal?"

"Sorry," she said and sounded like she meant it. "I'll be quiet and listen."

He almost chuckled, as she loved to gab, and he often hadn't been able to get a word in during their conversations. "I'm sure you know that doctors bill charges for Medicaid clients to the government. Your dad had a large number of clients who were legitimate Medicaid patients and billed accordingly. But he also billed for clients we've been tracking for suspicious charges."

She set down her cup and sat forward. "But why would

he do that? He didn't need the money. Or, at least, he didn't ever let on that he did."

"He led a pretty lavish lifestyle for a country doc."

"He had a huge inheritance from his family."

"Still, a plane, fancy cars, multiple properties. That all takes money. He could have run through his inheritance long ago."

"If you think that, why didn't you get a warrant to look at his banking records?"

"We tried, but the judge wanted additional information before granting our request. He did approve a warrant for your father's patient files, and I planned to serve his office manager with it tomorrow. But first I wanted to talk to you, as I'd hoped you would know where he was."

"You thought I was covering for him?" She recoiled. "With my relationship with him, how could you even think that?"

"I've been gone for a few years, Lex. I had no idea of your current status."

"He was still the same guy. Never available for Adam. Always slamming my profession whenever I ran into him. Being a nurse still wasn't worthy of the reputation he tried to cultivate. Only a doctor would do." Her voice hitched with emotion. "Even in his last words to me he mentioned his reputation."

"What? You didn't tell us that."

"Honestly, I forgot about it until now. Guess learning someone wants to kill you messes with your thoughts."

"In what context did he bring up his reputation?" he prodded.

"He said the envelope was my insurance and he should have done something, but then his voice fell off and he said, 'My reputation. Legacy.' Like these things stopped him from acting on whatever he was trying to tell me about."

"Legacy's an interesting choice of words."

"Is it?"

"He could have been talking about his inheritance. Or maybe he knew he wasn't going to make it and meant the money he was leaving behind."

"I don't know. I mean…" Tears flooded her eyes, and she looked up at the ceiling.

"I'm sorry, sugar."

"Don't call me that." She leveled her gaze on him. "You have no right."

The vehemence in her tone felt like a physical blow.

"I apologize," he said stiffly. "It's a habit, and I'll do my best not to do it again."

She ran a hand through her hair. "I overreacted. I guess I'm at the end of my rope."

"Maybe we should call it quits for the night," he said, though he really wanted to probe deeper.

"Sounds like a good idea." She raced away as if running from a dangerous foe and faced him at the exit. "Will you be attending the meeting tomorrow?"

"Yes."

She pulled open the door. The wind howled through the opening, but wasn't as frosty as her look. "Then I'll see you there."

He nodded. "Tessa should soon be done processing the phone left in your truck, so someone will stop by with it tonight."

"What? Why?"

"Because you'll need to keep that phone on you at all times in case the person who left it calls."

She clamped a hand over her mouth and her eyes opened wide. "I hadn't really thought about him calling me. Not sure why. I mean, he said he'd call with further instructions."

"You're still in shock from everything that's happened. Just promise me if the phone rings during the night that you'll call me right away and won't go anywhere. Not even with the deputy out front."

"Trust me. If I hear from this creep, I'll call."

With her vehement tone, he had no doubt she'd comply, though he still didn't like leaving her. But what choice did he have?

He exited, each step away from her raising his concern. He almost turned back until he saw his cousin Dylan climb out of the patrol car. Dylan was a top-notch deputy and Gavin could count on him to keep Lexie safe.

Gavin met his cousin at the curb. "I'm glad to see you on duty."

"This's crazy, isn't it?" Dylan settled his hands on his duty belt. "I hate that crimes like these are creeping into the county. Mostly big-city folks moving out here." He held up a hand. "No offense meant at that, bro. You're still one of us."

At least someone still thought of him that way. "You know I have a special interest in keeping Lexie safe, right?"

"Honestly, I wondered. What with your breakup and all, but then I saw you bring her home…" He shrugged.

"Water under the bridge." After seeing Lexie again tonight, Gavin knew their feelings most definitely *weren't* water under the bridge. They couldn't be or they wouldn't react so strongly to every little thing. But Dylan didn't need to know about any of that, so Gavin would keep up the pretense for as long as this investigation lasted.

"You have my cell number, right?" he asked.

Dylan nodded.

"Then call me if anything odd happens. Anything. I mean a cat jaywalks and you call me. Got it?"

Dylan eyed him. "We've been friends from birth, man, but when it comes to my job, my loyalty is to your dad."

"Fine, call him first and then me. 'Sides, you won't report a jaywalking cat to Dad unless you want to be razzed for life." Gavin punched his cousin's arm and stepped toward his vehicle.

He heard Dylan laughing and felt certain if a problem cropped up, he'd get a call.

Back at the ranch, Gavin wasn't surprised to see the family room light burning bright. His mother never went to bed until everyone under her roof was safe and sound in bed, and that meant him if he stayed with them while he was in town. He didn't need to wait to be asked. He knew she would insist, so he grabbed his suitcase and headed up the steps.

As he closed the front door, the wind jostled a tree ornament he'd made in first grade. He stared at the yarn-wrapped frame holding the picture with his gap-toothed smile. He still remembered presenting the package to his mom and dad. Remembered the love glowing in their eyes.

He sighed heavily. How had his life strayed so far from that? Living in a threadbare apartment in the city. Working every waking hour. Filled with emptiness much of the time, which was why he worked until he dropped from exhaustion. He'd wanted to be with his family. Had wanted to be with Lexie and see Adam grow up.

As it turned out, maybe it was a good thing he'd left. With the way shooting an innocent person had caused him to start controlling every little thing in life, he'd hate to think of how he'd treat any woman he was involved with. He'd be a real bear to live with, that was for sure. Lexie didn't deserve that. No woman did.

"Good gravy," his father shouted. "Can't those blasted reporters get anything right?"

Gavin set down his suitcase and joined his parents in time to see his dad turn off the TV then fling the remote at the end of the sofa.

His father tried to make sure the public received accurate facts about his department, but accurate often wasn't sensational, so reporters embellished the facts. Part of his concern was due to his being an elected official, but also because he, like every McKade before him, had great pride in law-enforcement work. Gavin respected that. Respected him as a sheriff. Gavin just couldn't work for him.

His father eyed him. "Lexie get home okay?"

Gavin nodded.

"And you checked the locks?"

He nodded again.

"They were secure?"

The warm nostalgia brought on by the ornament evaporated. "It's all been covered, Dad, so give it a rest."

His mother stood. "Why don't I get the two of you a nice cup of hot cocoa?"

Gavin really wanted to head up to his room, but his lack of visits was hard on his mother, so he smiled and nodded.

"Don't stand there like a guest," his dad said. "Take a seat."

Gavin dropped onto a leather club chair with worn patina. His dad had hit it on the head… He felt like a guest in his own home.

"S'posin while your mom is out of the room, you fill me in on why you're in town."

Gavin had hoped to wait until tomorrow when he wasn't as tired, but he might as well get it over with. He launched into the fraud story. "I read the news reports online about Dr. Grant's disappearance."

His dad planted his hands on his knees. "So you came here thinking your FBI training gave you skills to find the doctor where I failed."

"No. I'm mostly here to serve a warrant for his files, but I also planned to interview people. Not because I didn't think you did a thorough job, but because I'm lead on the investigation and *I* have to do a thorough job."

His dad watched him for a long moment. "Guess I taught you well, then."

"Yes." Gavin meant what he said. His dad was a fine sheriff.

"That why you were at the airstrip?"

"When I called Lexie, she said she would rather not be seen with me in town. She didn't want to deal with gossip about our breakup again."

"Makes sense, I suppose. What with the way gossip travels faster than that feisty stallion of yours. So what are your plans now?"

"I'll still serve the warrant tomorrow, and I was hoping to work with you on the murder investigation." Gavin held up his hand before his father could say a word. "Your investigation. Not mine. But we share information and keep each other in the loop about what we learn."

"Sounds reasonable."

Gavin had to work hard to keep his mouth from falling open. "Do you want to talk now about how we'll handle disagreements about procedure?"

"No need to talk about it. It's my county. My case. My way."

Right. He hadn't changed.

His mother joined them with a tray of steaming hot mugs and decorated sugar cookies. Gavin had meant to chug his cocoa once it was cool and head upstairs, but he never could resist Nana's Christmas cookies. He grabbed a bright yellow star and devoured it, then polished off a few more.

"Don't you eat in Houston?" his dad asked.

"No one makes cookies like Nana." Gavin resisted taking another one and blew on his mug to cool it.

"I saw your suitcase in the foyer," his mom said. "Glad I didn't have to convince you to stay."

"Why in the world would you have to convince the boy?" his dad asked.

She shook her head and launched into questions about Gavin's life in Houston. He talked with her on a regular basis, but not with his dad. Gavin figured she updated him, but he still seemed to be staring at Gavin. Not that he turned to check.

Once the cocoa was cool enough, he made quick work of drinking it and then started for the foyer. "I'm beat. See you all in the morning."

His mother came after him and drew him into a tight hug. "I'm so happy to have my firstborn under my roof again."

He peered at her, the guilt eating at his gut. "And I'm happy to see you, Mom. Real happy."

"Since you'll be staying for the unforeseen future, you know I'll make sure there's time for us to talk about everything before you leave, right?"

"I expected as much."

"Then spend some time figuring out how you're going to find your way back home."

Gavin glanced at his dad, who jerked his gaze away as

if not wanting to be caught watching. "I'll try, Mom, but you know it takes two. So far I haven't seen a change."

"Don't worry about him. I'm working on him, too. Just worry about yourself."

"Sound advice." He kissed her cheek. "Now, you should get some sleep."

He grabbed his suitcase and ran into his brother, Matt, on the upstairs landing.

"Saw your car out front," Gavin said. "Didn't know you were staying here, too."

"I'm pulling a second shift to help out and needed a fresh uniform to go out on patrol. Would be a waste of time to go home and change. So I took a quick shower to wake up, and Dad lent me one of his."

"Anything new since I left?" Gavin asked, thinking his brother would be more forthcoming than their father.

"Motor bike registration didn't pan out, but we'll get the word out via local channels and someone's bound to recognize it."

Gavin wished he wasn't so concerned with how laid-back his brother seemed. "Local channels?"

"Dad asked me to talk to the press and give them a picture of the bike." Matt shifted his duty belt higher. "He hates reporters, but if Dad finally does retire like he keeps claiming, I don't have his track record, so developing a relationship with the press is important."

"You're going to make a fine politician, little brother."

Matt's smile evaporated.

"I say something wrong?"

He looked around then lowered his voice. "Not sure I want all the politics. I like being in on the action, but I'm not a pencil pusher."

"But Dad—"

"Doesn't always know what's best for us." Matt crossed

his arms over a powerful chest built from hours of pumping iron. "You ought to know that."

"If that's how you feel, then you have to tell him."

"Right," Matt scoffed. "Like he and Mom could handle both their sons not toeing the line."

Great, now Gavin felt bad about this, too. Thanks to his leaving town, his brother couldn't say no to running for sheriff. Should have been Gavin's role, but even if he moved back to town, he felt the same way as Matt. He wasn't a pencil pusher, either. And thank goodness for that, because the world needed men and women to step up now more than ever to hunt down criminals before they hurt good people like Lexie.

SIX

Lexie sat in the school parking lot as she waited for Kendall and Adam to join her. She picked at a sliver of plastic peeling from the steering wheel on the old ranch pickup. Such an old beater. Lexie couldn't rely on the relic of a truck, so she had to get her own truck repaired ASAP. Turned out, she had plenty of time to do that since she wasn't going to work anytime soon. She didn't want this current predicament to follow her to the hospital, so she'd stopped by the ER to talk to her supervisor, who suggested Lexie take leave until everything was all sorted out.

She patted her jeans' pocket for about the zillionth time since leaving home to ensure the burner phone remained there. Having something bulky in her pocket constantly caught her attention when she'd just as soon forget that a criminal, likely a killer, would call. Her. Lexie Grant. A simple nurse in a simple town. Waiting to talk to a killer. Unbelievable.

Kendall stepped out the front door and held up her hand to keep Adam inside. A few moments later, she gestured again and the teen joined her, his gaze fixed on her and not his surroundings. He likely had a crush on Kendall. Tall and slender, the beautiful brunette took after her mother in her mannerisms, her hips swaying as she walked and looking nothing like the tough deputy Lexie knew her to be.

As the duo approached, Lexie pushed open the passenger door, the rusty hinges groaning with age. Adam climbed in, and Kendall poked her head inside.

"How did the morning go?" Lexie asked.

"Uneventful."

"Says you," Adam muttered. "You didn't have to take the math test."

A wide smile found Kendall's lips and she lifted her hand as if planning to pat Adam on the head, but then thought better of it and gestured behind the truck. "Officer Ellison's got you for the drive to the ranch. I have an errand to run, but I'll drop by Trails End this afternoon, and we can catch up."

"Sounds good," Lexie said.

Kendall closed the door and stepped back.

Adam shot Lexie a look. "You said we'd go home right after lunch."

"We were going to, but having deputies with us 24/7 is putting pressure on the sheriff department's schedule. So Walt called this morning to ask if we minded hanging at the ranch where we'll be safe."

"But I have a ton of homework, and my books are at home."

"Then we'll stop home to pick up your books first. Just let me tell Deputy Ellison so he doesn't wonder where we're going."

She quickly informed him of the change and then got the truck on the road with the deputy following.

Adam plugged in his earbuds, his music loud enough for her to hear across the seat. Normally she'd tell him to turn it down, but he'd had enough going on that she let it slide. After all, he wouldn't lose his hearing in the time it took for them to get home.

On the drive, the upcoming lunch invaded her thoughts. She had to admit she was glad for the extra time it would take to get Adam's homework, as it reduced the time she'd spend in Gavin's company. But she also had to admit that she was glad he'd cared enough to check the locks last night. Not that he cared enough to make her a priority and stay together, though. If he had, they'd likely be married now. Have a child on the way or already be parents.

She let herself imagine their life. Their home together. Their children. A happy family that included Adam flourishing with Gavin in the picture.

A loud blare of a train whistle jerked her from the daydream. She saw railroad crossing lights flashing ahead and the arm coming down. It was too late to stop, so she sped up and slipped safely under the arm.

She glanced back to find the deputy's car on the other side of the arm. A moment of fear took purchase, but she tamped it down and slowed to give him time to catch up after the train had passed. She rounded a curve and spotted a car parked on the shoulder. The trunk was open and an infant car seat sat on the ground near a woman resting her head against the rear fender.

Lexie could still hear the train rumbling down the tracks, so she pulled over. When the woman didn't move, Lexie's concern mounted. Was she hurt? Not conscious?

Adam looked up and took out an earbud. "What's going on?"

"A woman with a baby is having car trouble." Lexie shifted into Park. "She's not moving. I'm going to check on them."

"But won't Deputy Ellison do that?" Adam asked.

She told him about the train.

He bit his lip, last night still clearly affecting him. "Maybe we should wait for him."

Lexie unbuckled her belt. "This woman and child could need medical attention, Adam. Don't worry... I'll be fine."

She got out and approached the car, her gaze locked on the unmoving woman.

"Ma'am," Lexie said, but she didn't respond or acknowledge Lexie. "Ma'am?"

No response again, leaving Lexie unsettled. She eased closer when a gust of wind howled down the road, blowing the woman over.

A dummy. She's a dummy. This is a trap.

A rustling sound came from the woods. Lexie spun to see a man wearing a ski mask and black clothing dart out and race toward her. She bolted for her truck, but he launched himself into the air and tackled her. She hit the ground hard, gravel slicing into her cheek. She bucked and fought. Kicking. Twisting.

She heard footsteps racing toward them.

"Leave her alone!" Adam shouted.

"No!" Lexie yelled. "Go back to the car, Adam."

Her abductor faltered for a moment. Just long enough for her to shove him off, and he rolled into the ditch. She scrambled to her feet.

"Run!" she screamed at Adam.

They raced for the truck. She fumbled to get the door open. Saw her abductor lurch to his feet and start for them.

"C'mon, c'mon," she muttered as she finally pulled the latch and jumped inside. Adam hit the seat and jerked the door closed behind him.

"Lock your door," she shouted as she punched her button down in the old truck.

Sirens screamed behind them, coming closer. Had to be Deputy Ellison, but she wouldn't relax. Nor would she take her eyes off her attacker. She shifted the truck into gear, ready to take off if needed.

The masked man fled into the woods. She sighed with relief and slumped against the wheel.

If there were any doubts that the killer was coming back for her, they were long gone.

Her life really was on the line.

Gavin careened his SUV to a stop behind the road-block and jumped out. Multiple patrol cars lined the highway, their lights flashing. Ruth's ratty blue pickup sat behind a sedan parked on the shoulder, but Gavin couldn't see Lexie or Adam.

"Lexie," he shouted as he charged toward the barricade. "Where are you? Lexie, answer me!"

No response. Gavin vaulted the barricade and took off running. Matt stepped in front of him and planted his hands on Gavin's chest to stop him.

"Lexie. Is she—?"

"She's shaken up but fine. So is Adam. They're sitting in my patrol car."

Gavin tried to sidestep Matt to go to her, but his brother jumped in front of him. "She doesn't need to see you this upset. Take a minute to calm down."

Gavin had to see Lexie to be sure she was okay, but Matt was right. His distress would only serve to raise her anxiety. He took a breath. Then another. Tension flowed out on every exhalation and his heart started beating again. Okay, fine, maybe that was an exaggeration, but when he'd heard about her attack on the ranch scanner, it had *felt* like his heart had stopped dead in his chest.

"Tell me what happened," he demanded.

Matt arched a brow, likely at Gavin's tone, but he quickly filled him in on what had just transpired.

Gavin's fists tightened more with each detail of the chain of events leading up to the man with the ski mask charging after Lexie and then escaping into the woods when reinforcements arrived.

"Any hope of catching this jerk?"

"We have deputies scouring the area, but Ellison heard a car take off from behind the woods."

"You think he had a different getaway car parked on the old logging trail?"

Matt nodded. "No witnesses, of course, as the area isn't inhabited. Makes this a perfect location for an abduction."

"You run the plates on the abandoned car?" Gavin asked.

"It was stolen in Prineville," Matt replied. "I'll look into the vehicle's owners for any possible connection. Also check for any video of the area where it was stolen and talk to any witnesses."

Gavin clapped his brother on the shoulder. "Wouldn't expect any less of you."

Matt gave a firm nod of thanks. "Tessa's on her way, too. Not that there's much here to process."

"The attacker had to know Lexie's schedule if he was lying in wait near her house."

"You think he's been watching her?"

Though Gavin hated the thought of the creep keeping eyes on her, he nodded.

Matt grimaced. "We need to increase our protection detail."

"I got that covered. As soon as I heard the news on the scanner, I decided I'm going to insist on her staying at the ranch with us."

"C'mon, bro. You know Lexie. After her dad's heavy-handed behavior, she's not about to agree to that." Matt eyed him. "You never would have thought to make such a demand before you left town. Houston has changed you."

"Then I'll ask her. Is she free to leave?"

Matt nodded and Gavin pushed past him, not bothering to wait for his brother's permission to step onto his crime scene. Gavin needed proof that Lexie and Adam weren't injured. They both still had a huge part of his heart. If his reaction to hearing about her near abduction told him anything, Lexie claimed a far bigger part than he'd thought when he'd arrived in town yesterday. So how in the world did he handle that while keeping her safe and finding her father's killer?

First step was to remain calm. Let her see that he was capable of taking care of her. That she and her brother wouldn't come to any harm under his watch. The rest he'd have to play by ear.

At the patrol car, he squatted down by the open door. "Are you okay?"

She nodded, but it was wooden and controlled, her hands clasped together in a death grip. Her jeans were torn, revealing bloody scraped knees, and the side of her face was red and raw. The thought of some jerk putting his hands on her sent his anger soaring, but he tamped it down. Seeing how upset she was, he decided he couldn't add to her turmoil right now by suggesting she stay at the ranch with them. He would take her back there for lunch, and then, when she was more relaxed, he'd bring it up.

"If you're ready," he said. "I'll drive you to Trails End."

She kept looking at him, her eyes dark and worried, but a note of defiance also lingered. "I can't leave Ruth's truck sitting alongside the road."

"We can give Matt a key and he'll make sure it's taken to Ruth's place."

"Then how will I get home?"

"I took your truck in for repair and cleaning this morning. It's at Trails End, waiting for you."

She faced Adam. "I need a private word with Gavin. I'll be right back."

Gavin moved out of the way, and she climbed out to step to the rear of the car. "I'm still a little freaked out, so I'm glad for the ride and for Matt taking care of Ruth's truck. Even for you having my truck repaired as long as you give me the bill. But I want to be sure your offer is only for lunch, and you're not going to suggest we stay at the ranch with you all, because that's not happening."

"Not even if it means Adam is safe?" He regretted his words the minute they came out as she closed her eyes and fisted her hands.

He hadn't meant to play into her fear, but she needed to recognize their extreme danger.

Matt stepped up to them. "What about staying in one of the rental cabins?"

"Good idea," Gavin said. "You wouldn't have to be under the same roof as me, but you'd be on a secure property with all of us available to help. With our past relationship, no one would think you'd want to stay anywhere near me."

"The cabin sounds good," she said, but didn't sound convinced.

"Since we're close to Ruth's ranch we can pick up your things right now," he offered, as he wasn't taking any chances that during lunch she'd realize the plan would keep them in close proximity and she'd change her mind.

"It's okay with me." Matt peered at Lexie. "But we'll

need your clothes bagged so Tessa can swab them for DNA. I can send the bag with Gavin."

"Is that really necessary?" she asked.

"Whether you like it or not, Lex." Gavin pulled his shoulders back. "You have a killer tracking you. If we can find his DNA on your clothes, we'll be one step closer to putting him behind bars."

Lexie sat next to Adam in the back of Gavin's SUV. Gavin had opened the front door for her, and while she'd been tempted to slide in next to him, she'd needed to be close to her brother. To take his hand and assure him that they would be okay. Not an easy thing to do when she no longer believed it.

What was to stop the killer from tracking her? Was he watching them right now?

She looked out the back window, searching for any vehicle tailing them. Then she remembered with Matt closing the road it would be impossible. But still, the feeling of someone watching didn't go away. She was likely overreacting, but fear did that to a person.

True, she found comfort in Gavin's strong, steady presence and she could choose to focus on that, but then she'd have to think about him more often, and she didn't need another reason to do so.

A patrol car came roaring toward them, lights and siren blaring. She caught sight of Sheriff McKade behind the wheel. If he recognized Gavin's vehicle, he didn't show it by waving or slowing to talk to them.

Adam shivered, and she tightened her grip on his hand. He may be fourteen and want to act all grown up, but he recognized the stakes here just as she did.

"Nothing to be worried about, bud. We're safe."

"Now, sure." His chin quivered. "But then what?"

"Then we'll stay with the McKades, and they'll take care of us."

"At the ranch with him?" He pointed at Gavin's head. "No way."

"We'll have our own cabin."

"But *he'll* still be around."

"You know we all care about you and will do our very best for you," Gavin said.

"Right." Adam rolled his eyes. "Like you actually care about us."

"That was rude, Adam," Lexie said, even though deep down she felt the same way. "It's our safest option right now, and I need you to make the best of it. For me, okay?"

He gave a sullen nod.

"Now, apologize."

"Sorry," he said, but she was sure he didn't mean it.

"I should have asked before we left the pickup behind," Gavin said, obviously ignoring the whole thing. "But do you still have the phone on you?"

She glanced at Adam but he seemed oblivious to their conversation. Still, she was thankful that Gavin was sensitive enough not to call it a burner phone to remind Adam of last night. She patted her pocket to assure him.

"And no calls?"

She shook her head and sat back for the last quarter mile to the ranch she'd called home since her teen years. Staring out the window, she watched the wide-open fields pass by, the many oil pump jacks dipping in rhythm and groaning with the exertion. Her father had inherited a small oil company, Grant Oil, and he'd once traded on his relationship as Ruth's brother-in-law to ask her for the rights to search for oil under her property. Thankfully, Ruth hadn't needed the money to keep the ranch going, unlike so many of their neighbors.

Their corral at the road soon came into view. Four horses grazed in the space where Misty would normally be located this time of day, but her horse was still at the McKade ranch. Lexie couldn't continue to trade on the McKade generosity in caring for and feeding Misty. Ruth's ranch hand would arrive later in the day to tend to the horses, and she'd call him to pick up Misty and schedule overtime with him to do the morning chores, too.

Gavin turned the car onto the winding gravel driveway lined with tall trees, and Lexie sighed out a breath when the familiar ranch house surrounded by Ruth's large flower beds came into view. This home had become a sanctuary after she'd lost her mother and her father had turned his back on them. She wished she could stay here tonight with Adam, but just like she'd asked her brother to do, she'd make the best of things.

They all climbed out and headed up the walkway lined with candy-cane lights. A large nativity set that had been in the family for generations sat by an even bigger manger, adding to Lexie's feeling of security but also reminding her that she hadn't prayed for God's help in many years.

Her pastor had taught her as a child to think of God like a father. A heavenly one, but a father nonetheless. She'd once found that comforting. Until her father's abandonment. Then she'd chalked up her belief in God loving people unconditionally as foolish childhood musings.

So why bother asking Him for something when for all she knew He'd abandoned her, too?

She unlocked the door, and as she pushed it open, she glanced back at Adam. "Though I hope we won't need it, I want you to pack for a few days at least. And grab all of your books so…"

His face blanched and he took a step back.

"What is it?" she asked.

He pointed at the door.

She turned, peered into the family room and gasped.

"No, oh, no…" She backed away, bumping into Adam. "Not here, too."

SEVEN

Gavin pushed past the pair to look into the house. Furniture, books and papers were scattered across the floor.

"Back to the car." Gavin drew his gun and hurried them to his SUV while keeping his head on a swivel.

Once settled inside, he dialed his father, who he knew was just down the road. Gavin kept checking out the windows even when his father answered.

Gavin explained their discovery. "I don't know if they're still here, but I won't leave Lexie and Adam in the car alone to clear the house."

"On my way," his dad responded.

Gavin stowed his phone and peered at Lexie. "We'll wait here for Dad to check the house."

"And then what?" Lexie's voice rose sky-high. "Dig through the mess to find things to pack? To find Adam's books?"

Gavin gave Lexie a pointed look then cut his gaze toward the boy sitting wide-eyed beside her, his focus fixed straight ahead.

She clamped a hand over her mouth then dropped it and took Adam's hand. "We're okay. Help is on the way."

He gave her an as-if look and slumped in the seat. Gavin didn't miss the shaking of the boy's knees or the trembling of his chin. When Gavin and Lexie had started dating, Adam had already thought of himself as the man of the family, protecting Ruth and Lexie. Gavin had thought it was cute back then, but now Adam was likely blaming himself for not being up to the task and for being afraid, too.

And on top of it, Gavin had put this kid through so much. He wished he could fix things between them, but he had no idea how.

"The dogs," Adam suddenly cried out. "They didn't meet us at the door."

"I'm sure they're fine," Lexie said, but Gavin heard the underlying doubt in her tone.

Sirens cut through the air and Adam shot forward. He was wound as tight as a penned-up bull.

"That'll be Dad," Gavin said, though it was obvious.

The patrol car pulled up alongside them and his father jumped out, his hand clamped on his holster. Gavin admired his dad for staying in great shape and, for once, had to admit he was happy to see him.

He drew his weapon and signaled for Gavin to stay put as he started for the door. Gavin hated sitting back and waiting, but he had to think of Lexie and Adam. If the intruder was still inside, he could come barreling out of the house. Gavin needed to remain alert.

He released the strap on his holster and rested his hand on the butt of his gun. Time ticked by slowly. Gavin's pulse throbbed in his neck, and not until his father stepped out did he start to breathe normally.

"You two stay here." He crossed over to his father.

He holstered his weapon but, just like Gavin, he didn't let down his guard. "Found the dogs drugged in the kitchen. They're breathing, but we need to get a vet out here. And the whole place has been ransacked."

Gavin glanced back at the car and found Adam's face plastered to the window. "Lexie and Adam are going to lose it when they see the place, but they'll really freak when they hear about Salt and Pepper."

His dad gave a solemn nod. "Looks like the intruder was looking for information."

"You know," Gavin said, "if the information the killer wants is worth killing over, then I have to think it's valuable and someone else is looking for it, too."

"Possible. At least, we can't rule it out. Once Tessa is done down the road, I'll get her over here to process the scene." He dug out his phone. "Gonna be a long afternoon here."

"We can't leave Lexie and Adam sitting in the car that long, but I don't want to bring them back here later to get their things and risk exposing them to danger."

"Agreed," his father said. "I have booties in the car. We can escort them through the house to minimize contamination, and they can pack a bag."

Gavin nodded. "You take Adam. He's royally mad at me for leaving, so it would be better for you to help him."

"And Lexie isn't?"

"She's mad, all right, but she's older and can handle it better." At least, Gavin hoped that was the case.

Gavin escorted the pair to the house, where his dad waited with a box of booties. After they'd all covered their shoes, his father headed into the house with Adam.

"Ready?" Gavin asked Lexie.

She stepped inside and gasped. Gavin stepped up to her and took her hand, not caring how she might react to his touch. Her gaze searched his for a long moment, but then she eased closer to him.

"I hate that you have to go through this." He continued to hold tightly to her hand. "If I could take it away, I would in a heartbeat. You know that, right?"

"I know that's who you are. The brave defender who wants to help others in need."

It's more than that—it's you, he thought to say, but kept his mouth shut, as he had no right to tell her that. No right to even be thinking that. Not unless he was going to commit to staying in Lost Creek and hold her hand for a lifetime. Something he just couldn't do.

On the drive to Trails End, Lexie patted the burner phone to confirm she'd moved it to her clean jeans when she'd bagged her other ones for Matt. She rested her head on the seat and closed her eyes. The attack by the roadside weighed heavily on her mind, but even more, she couldn't let go of the pictures of her home, her sanctuary, torn apart.

How was she going to tell Ruth about the dogs and the mess? Thankfully, Dr. Wilson believed Salt and Pepper had been given a mild sedative and would be fine. Just to be sure, he'd taken them to his practice so his staff could keep an eye on them. Lexie had thought to call Ruth, but she wasn't about to ruin her aunt's vacation. There was nothing she could do here, anyway, and hopefully this would be over before she was due back two days from now.

The car came to a stop and Lexie was surprised to see they'd reached the ranch. Once Tessa had arrived at Ruth's place, Walt had departed, and his car, along with a patrol car, was now parked outside the ranch house. The front door opened and Winnie and Betty stepped out.

Lexie was glad to see them both, but after the recent incidents, she had to force a smile for them. She waited for Adam to join her and tried to put her arm around his back, but he shrugged it off. Something had changed while he'd packed. He'd gone from being afraid to being mad. Once they were alone at the cabin, she planned to have a long talk with him.

"Cabin's ready, Gavin," Winnie called out. "Why don't you take Lexie's and Adam's things over there?"

Gavin peered at Lexie and looked like he didn't want to leave her, but she needed him to go. She'd already let him hold her hand, and she could only imagine what more she might allow if he stayed nearby. Maybe hold her. Even kiss her.

A far-too-dangerous temptation for her peace of mind.

"Do you mind?" she asked.

"Not at all." He smiled. "You and Adam go inside, and I'll be back in a jiffy."

Lexie and Adam climbed the stairs.

"C'mon, Adam." Betty opened the front door. "Let's you and I head into the kitchen and have lunch together."

"What are we having?" he asked.

"Beef stew and some lovely rolls I baked this morning. And if after that you still have room, I've set aside a plate of Christmas cookies with your name on them."

He stepped inside and Lexie hoped he could actually eat after everything that had just happened. And she was grateful that Walt had arranged for Adam to eat in the kitchen so he wouldn't have to hear the upcoming discussion.

"Now, what about you?" Winnie asked. "Hungry?"

Lexie shook her head and felt tears pricking her eyes.

Winnie gathered Lexie in a hug and didn't say a word. She had open arms for anyone in need, reminding Lexie of her own mother. A trauma nurse, just like Lexie, her mom's heart had been the size of Texas, and her nurturing spirit had drawn everyone to her. She'd also been a spitfire in the ER. Lexie tried to emulate her mother and hoped she succeeded.

"I'm sorry for everything that's happening, sweetheart." Winnie pulled back and studied Lexie's face. "I think we'll all rest easier with you staying in a cabin. I heard Gavin pacing at all hours of the night, and I suspect he was worrying about you and Adam."

Lexie had to admit it felt good to think he was looking out for her again even if she didn't believe he'd stay by her side for the long run, but she wouldn't share that with Winnie. "He was probably up thinking about his investigation."

"Hogwash." She stepped back. "It's plain to see he still cares for you."

"Good gravy, Winnie," Walt called out from inside. "Let little Lexie get in here and close the door before we pay to heat the entire state of Texas."

Winnie shook her head. "You can still join us for lunch in case your appetite returns. And don't forget what I said about Gavin. He does care for you."

Before Lexie could argue more, Winnie led the way to the dining room, where Matt and Walt sat at the table Lexie had dined at nearly every Sunday after she and Gavin had gotten serious.

"Let me get lunch on the table," Winnie said.

"Can I help?" Lexie offered.

"I wouldn't hear of it. Have a seat and I'll be right back." Winnie went through the swinging door to the kitchen.

By the time Lexie sat, Gavin joined them. He went straight for a carafe of coffee.

"Want some?" he asked Lexie.

She nodded.

After he filled a mug to the brim, she cupped her

hands around it for warmth and shifted her gaze to Matt. "Anything new in the investigation?"

He nodded. "We located the dirt bike owner. An Odon Walmet. He claims the bike was stolen, but he has a sketchy past that involved extortion."

"And he doesn't have a solid alibi for last night." Walt slid a photo across the table to her. "Could he be your guy?"

She studied the pockmarked face with its scraggly beard and skin toughened from the Texas sun. "I didn't get a look at the killer's face, so I can't say. He looks thin, though, and the shooter was thin. Do you have a full body shot?"

Matt shook his head. "No, but I talked to him and he fits the build you described last night."

"Does he have any connection to my dad?"

"He's a patient, but hasn't seen your father for years." Matt slipped the picture back into the folder. "Since we can't rule him out yet, I'll continue looking into him. If it turns out he's a viable suspect, I'll arrange a voice lineup for you to determine if his voice matches the killer's."

Lexie was about to comment on the lineup, when Winnie came in and placed a big pot of stew on the table. The savory scent of garlic and onions filled the air and got Lexie's taste buds working again.

"If one of you will ladle out the stew, I'll be right back with rolls Betty just took out of the oven." Winnie didn't wait for a response, but bustled to the kitchen.

Needing to keep busy, Lexie stood and filled Walt's bowl with meat and vegetables covered in rich brown gravy.

"Thank you," he said. "I believe we should focus on figuring out what your daddy was involved in and what was in that envelope to warrant murder."

"I'm hoping the answer can be found in his patient files," Gavin said.

"Since that's the only real motive we have right now for murdering Dr. Grant, I have to concur," Walt said.

Lexie ladled an overflowing scoop of stew into Gavin's bowl. "I was planning to go to Dad's house and office today to look at his records."

"You can still go, but I'll be escorting you." Gavin's tone was unyielding.

She paused, ladle midair, to study him. Had Gavin always been bossy and controlling like her daddy—like his father—but love had blinded her to it?

No. He'd never pushed her around, and now that it seemed to be a big part of his personality, she didn't like it. Not one bit. But she wasn't a fool. She wanted to be safe and wouldn't argue about being accompanied.

She could and would argue about who did the accompanying, though. "I'm sure you have things you need to do for your investigation. Perhaps Matt or your dad could escort me."

He folded his arms across the broad chest she'd rested her head against so many times and issued her a nonverbal challenge. "It has to be me."

She wanted to cross her arms, too, but she still held the ladle. "Why?"

"Remember I mentioned the warrant last night? Well, I can't have you going through files that I have legal authority to seize."

Right. The investigation, not her safety, was his priority. Even more reason not to go with him. "But I—"

"Should just agree. We can review the files together. He was your father, and you may notice something I miss."

Her broken heart told her to continue arguing, but

logic said it was time to give in. "I didn't really know him any better than you, but I want to see the files, so I guess we'll go together." She grabbed Matt's bowl. "So let's agree on a protection plan for Adam and me, and then we can head over to Dad's house."

Spoon in hand, Walt paused in lifting it to his mouth. "As I mentioned this morning, my resources are tapped out, but with you staying here, that will help."

"I'm thankful you agreed." Gavin's words came out choked and reminded Lexie of Winnie's recent comment.

After their breakup, Lexie had often imagined, maybe even wished, Gavin's suffering equaled or exceeded hers. Now that she could hear his pain, she was sorry for thinking that way. She shouldn't wish him or anyone else emotional distress, and she was ashamed she'd done so.

Winnie stepped into the room with a basket of golden rolls, the smell of warm yeast overpowering the stew. She handed them to Walt, but her gaze roamed between Gavin and Lexie. She was such an intuitive woman that even if she hadn't been in the room, she noticed the emotions zinging between the two of them.

Oblivious to the undercurrent of tension, Walt helped himself to a roll and passed the basket to Gavin. "I don't want you to think by staying at the ranch that I'm leaving you high and dry. I'll keep a deputy in reserve if needed, and I'll continue to have off-duty deputies who volunteer their time escort Adam to school and spend the day with him." He cleared his throat. "And Matt and I can fill in for short time frames, but each hour we do will take us away from the investigation, so I'd rather curtail that as much as possible."

Lexie spooned her own stew then gave Walt an earnest smile. "I really appreciate all you're doing for us."

"You're practically family, Lexie. I can do no less." He pressed a warm hand over hers.

Practically. The word stuck in her throat and she couldn't respond. She'd been so close to being a Mc-Kade. To having this amazing family adopt her through marriage. It would have been so wonderful. Not only for her, but also for Adam. Having such strong men to serve as role models on a daily basis at this vulnerable stage in his development would have been so incredible. Gavin could have been such an important part of Adam's life. If only…

Stop.

It wasn't going to happen. Not now. Not in the future.

"Time to get some of this hearty stew in your stomach." Winnie took Lexie by the shoulder and settled her in the chair. She squeezed her hand before releasing her. "I'll leave you to your discussion, but don't get so caught up that you forget to enjoy your food while it's still warm."

Lexie smiled up at the woman who would have been a wonderful mother-in-law, then quickly turned her attention to the stew to keep her wayward emotions from spiraling out of control. There was no point in thinking about what could have been, as God had made it clear that such a traditional family was out of the question for her right now. Maybe for forever. She just didn't know.

They ate in silence and Lexie suspected they were all thinking about how to proceed after the near abduction and break-in at Ruth's house.

After a few minutes, Matt's spoon clanked on his bowl as he raised his napkin to wipe his mouth. "We can't all look at records, so we should come up with a suspect list to spread the work around. I'd start with guys in the area who have the skills needed to blow up a plane."

"The ATF report said dynamite was used for the charge,

which is far too common round these parts to track down," Walt said. "And the device had a simple timer with an action circuit controlled by his phone."

"Can't buy a circuit like that around here, but it can be purchased online and won't narrow down a suspect list," Gavin said. "So we're better off looking at people with explosives experience and a basic knowledge of electrical wiring."

"Good thinking, son," Walt said. "There's Earl Clark over at Clem's Garage. Clark knows about wiring from working on cars. Plus he used to handle demo for an oil company. He also fits the killer's build."

"Know him, Lex?" Matt asked.

She shook her head. "Jose fixes all of our vehicles."

Gavin pulled a small notepad from his pocket and jotted down the name. "We should also consider Norbert and his son Freddie Nash, who live up near the county line. I remember from hauling them in a few times for drug possession that they both have electrical skills. Plus Norbert handled explosives."

"If they're involved, their drug use could indicate a syndicate," Matt said. "Though there's never been any suggestion that these guys are more than low-level users."

"It's common for drug users to escalate and often move into peddling drugs to pay for their habit," Gavin stated, noting the names on his pad.

Matt's gaze turned pensive. "That's true, but is it true in this situation?"

Lexie couldn't believe the direction the discussion had gone. "Surely you don't think my dad was a drug dealer."

"At this point we have to entertain all possible leads," Gavin said. "And illegal drugs can easily mean a syndicate. Plus drugs are always a strong motive for murder."

"Let's not forget Silas Ross," Matt chimed in, changing the focus. "He has a record, too, and last I heard he was still working in explosives with one of the oil companies. I haven't seen him around lately, so maybe he's moved."

Walt nodded. "You know Silas or the Nash men, Lexie?"

She shook her head. "It's great to have names, but why would any of these men want to kill Dad other than a drug connection, which, honestly, I find hard to believe?"

"Well, I'm still thinking the syndicate is related to the Medicaid fraud," Gavin said. "And the killer somehow learned your dad was using their social security numbers to defraud the government. Maybe more."

"Best way to figure that out is bring them into the office for a little one-on-one." Walt pushed to his feet. "I'll get interviews set up, and if they don't have an alibi for the near abduction and the time of the murder, then I'll press for their connection with Dr. Grant."

"And I'll arrange the voice lineup for Walmet," Matt added and stood, too. "We can do the same thing for the others if their alibis don't pan out."

Walt nodded and turned his attention to Lexie. "If all goes well this afternoon, you could soon be hearing the voice of your father's killer."

Goes well? Lexie shuddered. How could hearing the voice of the man who'd killed her dad be considered a good thing?

EIGHT

Gavin dropped the folder on Dr. Grant's desk. He'd been sitting next to Lexie for an hour, reading her father's financial records. He was in his element here. Doing what he'd trained to do. So why was he having to work so hard to focus? Was it the sweet scent of Lexie's vanilla shampoo bringing back so many memories? Or the warmth of her body reminding him of how wonderful it had once felt to hold her? Especially after he'd argued with his father or had a miserable day.

He missed her big-time. He sighed, drawing her attention.

"Mind scooting a little further away?" she asked pointedly.

"Sorry—can't," he replied, though he really wasn't sorry, as he loved being close to her. He'd felt that way since they started dating. "I have to see the records, too."

Her chin went up in her usual attempt to make herself appear taller and more formidable. She obviously felt a need to defend herself like she'd done with her father. Gavin didn't want to be compared to her father. Not ever. But he'd acted like her dad. Moving to Houston. Not talking to her since. Then coming back here and telling her what to do without any regard to her feelings.

But she's in danger.

Not an excuse and he knew it. It was all about his need to take charge and keep his finger on every action in his life to stop bad things from happening.

Look how well that's been working.

She suddenly cleared her throat and pushed back from the desk. "It's clear that Dad wasn't destitute, so maybe this has nothing to do with money at all."

Right, business. They were there to work, nothing personal between them anymore, and he needed to remember that. "Don't be so quick to jump to that conclusion, Lex. These statements are from the last six months, so we have no way of knowing where the money came from without accessing older records."

"But there isn't anything else in his file."

"His bank will have more." Gavin closed the drawer.

"You can't get a warrant for them, though, right?"

"Not at this point, but hopefully I'll find enough information at his office to satisfy the judge."

Lexie's phone rang from her coat pocket and she fished it out. She got a puzzled look on her face, but answered.

"Hello?" A frown soon drew down her very kissable lips.

Don't go there, man.

She picked at a sliver of leather curling up on her father's desk blotter, her frown deepening as she listened. "Thank you, Mike."

Mike? Maybe Mike Alexander, her father's attorney.

"His will," she said, confirming Gavin's suspicion. "Does it contain his burial wishes?"

She pressed the leather back down as if trying to repair it and her life.

"Then I appreciate the call, but honestly, I have no interest in hearing about what Dad wanted to have done with his worldly possessions." She hung up and stowed her phone.

"Mike Alexander?" Gavin asked.

She nodded. "He wanted me to stop by for a reading of the will. He said it was kind of complicated, and I should hear about it sooner rather than later." She turned to peer out the window overlooking a lush lawn. "I haven't even made funeral arrangements yet. I'm not at all ready to hear what Dad wanted done with his stuff."

Gavin thought the will could give them insight into her father's thoughts and maybe his finances, but she was in no frame of mind to be pushed into a reading. He could also request a warrant for the will, but at this juncture, they didn't have enough probable cause for the judge to approve the document.

Hoping the office visit would turn something up, he got up and stacked several boxes filled with records that he planned to take into evidence. "Let me get these boxes out to the car, and then we'll head over to his practice."

Lexie nodded but continued to stare into space, so he carried the first load outside. The crisp northerly wind swept over the area, reminding him that Christmas was just weeks away and he hadn't even considered where he'd be for the holiday. He'd spent the last two years working. His life had taken such a sharp turn away from family and friends. How pitiful was that, and how in the world had he let it happen so easily?

He settled the boxes in his vehicle with a pensive sigh. Had he been wrong in leaving town? Could he have survived under his dad's thumb? No. No way. He shook his head and went back inside.

Lexie jumped, but didn't look up at him.

He desperately wanted to console her, but there was no point in trying to offer comfort when his touch would only make things worse. But, man, what he wouldn't give to have her in his arms one more time.

Shaking off those foolhardy notions, he picked up the final box. "This is the last one, and we should get going, as Helen is waiting for us."

"Helen Byrum," Lexie said as if reminding herself of the name of her father's office manager. "I haven't been to the practice in years, and I can only imagine what Dad told her about why he didn't live with Adam and me."

Not something Gavin thought was a good idea to dwell on. "Let me get this last box in the car and then I'll come back for you."

He quickly departed before she asked about his reasoning and he'd have to tell her that he needed his hands free to go for his gun if necessary. Before returning to the house, he made a quick sweep of the area, checking shadows and blind spots. Convinced there was no immediate danger, he escorted her to the car and got them on the road.

He didn't speak for the entire drive, as after the attempted abduction yesterday, he had to keep his gaze moving over the area and checking the mirrors. Even when they hit Lost Creek, a town he'd always considered safe despite it being the largest city in Lake County, he searched storefronts and vehicles.

Satisfied by what he was seeing, he parked in front of the office. "I'll come around to open your door. Stay close to me."

She nodded, but looked like she'd swallowed some bitter medicine. Still, she'd listened and remained by his side until they stepped inside the office. Lexie greeted Helen as Gavin turned the door lock behind them and went straight to the blinds to close them.

Though he knew Helen, he displayed his credentials for her. "Are you alone?"

"Yes," she replied.

"You don't mind if I take a look, do you?"

"What's going on?" she asked.

"Let me look around and then I'll explain." Gavin stepped through the open door leading to a hallway with three exam rooms and several offices.

How many times had he as a kid come down this hall to have something stitched up or to get an X-ray for an injured limb from horseback riding or sports? Twice needing a cast, one time suffering a concussion. Now here he was, checking each room and the bathrooms for a killer. Surreal for sure.

On his way back down the hallway, he heard Helen talking about him.

"Seems like he's forgotten all about being one of your dad's patients," she grumbled. "Got to be a big shot in Houston, I guess."

Why was everyone thinking that? He was just doing his job. Sure, maybe he was more formal, more in control, but his job required it.

He stepped into the small waiting area and Helen eyed him through thick glasses. She sat behind the reception desk, her lips puckered. Was this the same woman who'd given him lollipops after his appointments? Maybe she was right. Maybe he was acting too tight-laced for the small-town atmosphere.

"I'm sorry to be so terse, Helen." He smiled amicably. "Is there a place we can all sit down to talk and I can explain?"

"My office." She stood. "Follow me."

She clipped down the hall and they trailed her to the smaller of the two offices. She dropped behind her desk that was neat and organized. Lexie settled in a chair facing the desk.

Gavin remained standing and pulled the warrant from his pocket. "As you can tell, I'm not here on a social visit but official business. I have a warrant authorizing me to seize Dr. Grant's records."

Her thick eyebrows rose above her glasses as she held out her hand for the document. She took her time reviewing it before looking up.

"Do you understand the request?" he asked.

She crossed her arms. "We may be a small office in rural Texas, but this isn't the first court order we've ever received to produce records. What are you looking for?"

"I'm afraid I can't divulge that."

"But you must think Doc did something illegal or you wouldn't have a warrant."

He nodded but said nothing.

"You're not going to tell me because you think I'm in on whatever it is you hope to find."

Again, Gavin couldn't deny it, so he didn't speak.

She looked at Lexie. "You knew about this?"

Lexie nodded.

"Your father's not even in the ground and you can come here demanding such a thing?"

Lexie recoiled. "We hope the files will help us find who killed him."

"But you don't think either of us did anything illegal, do you?"

Lexie shrugged.

"Tell me this isn't happening." Helen clamped a hand over her mouth.

Gavin would like to ease her mind, but if Dr. Grant was defrauding the government, she could very well know about it. "As the warrant says, I'll be taking all patient files and billing records."

She crossed her arms. "I'll help you with the files, but billing records aren't kept here. Doc had a local gal do all the billing electronically, and she gave the files to him every month."

"I hope you'll understand that my job requires me to search the office anyway."

"I understand."

"So you never saw the bills?" Lexie sounded surprised, but she didn't have much to do with her father, so it made sense that she didn't know how he ran his practice.

Helen sniffed. "Only ever saw one if a patient put it in front of my face to ask a question, and I referred him to the biller. I was always glad I didn't have to deal with any of that. I'd hate to know which of my neighbors didn't pay Doc on time."

"Did you not handle the office finances at all?" Gavin asked.

"Doc took care of all of that. I gave him expense reports at the end of the month and he paid the bills."

"Sounds like my dad," Lexie said. "Keeping the money all under his purview."

Helen peered up at Gavin. "Before we go any further, suppose you answer a question for me. Do I need an attorney?"

"Did you do anything wrong?"

"No, of course not."

"Then you shouldn't need an attorney."

Lexie peered up at him, a deep scowl on her face. She thought he was being too harsh with Helen, but he was simply doing his job. Sure, if the same situation occurred when he'd been a deputy, he might have softened the blow, but he wasn't a rural county deputy any longer. He was an FBI agent with strict standards to uphold.

Okay, fine, he could relax a bit, but he wouldn't. That led to thinking about this town. The people. His family and Lexie, when he needed to think only about putting the killer behind bars and bringing this Medicaid investigation to a swift and thorough closure.

"Can you think of anyone who might want to kill Dad?" Lexie asked, maybe because she felt a need to step in before Helen got mad.

"You know your dad," Helen replied. "He could be hard to get along with at times. But his patients loved him." She frowned. "Well, maybe not all of them, I suppose."

"Are you thinking of someone in particular?" Gavin asked, trying not to sound too eager.

"Three people actually. The month before Doc went missing. He refused to fill their prescriptions and they stormed out of here. Next thing I knew, they canceled future appointments, and we got requests from the Lowell Clinic for the patient files."

Gavin's interest perked up at the clinic name, as Dr. Lowell was another potential suspect in the Medicaid fraud. "The same doctor for all three patients?"

She nodded.

"And you didn't think that was odd?" Gavin asked, as he sure did.

"This isn't like the big city, where you can choose from a long list of doctors. We only have two GPs in the county and Lowell is the closest."

He took out his notebook. "I'd like the patient names."

"Look, your warrant doesn't force me to give out their names, so I can't do that." Helen bit her lip. "But it does give you access to the schedule, where you might notice a few canceled appointments."

She pushed an appointment book toward Gavin and he picked it up to flip through the pages. He ran a finger down each day until he hit on the first crossed-off names: Rex Sanderson and Billy Howard. He jotted the names in his notebook and continued down the list until he found the third name and had to work hard to stifle his enthusiasm.

He tapped the calendar and peered at Helen. "Billy Howard, Rex Sanderson and Silas Ross. These are the patients you were referring to?"

Helen nodded. "But remember, I didn't say anything."

"Silas," Lexie said. "Didn't you mention—?"

"I assume I'll find the patient files in your records," Gavin interrupted before Lexie mentioned they'd already put Silas on the suspect list at lunch. Gavin added a pointed look to tell her to keep it to herself.

"Don't worry," Helen replied. "The files are right where I put them."

Perfect. Now all Gavin had to do was pack up the records, cross-reference the names and addresses with his list of suspicious Medicaid clients, and they could very well have a suspect angry enough to commit murder.

NINE

Thankfully, the doc only kept patient files for the current year at the office and the remaining files were already boxed and in a secure storage facility, limiting the number of files that Gavin had to pack up. He was able to load them into his SUV, put a seal on the office door and the storage unit, and then get Lexie back to the ranch within a few hours.

He still had to go back into town and serve the warrant on the woman with the billing records. He wouldn't expose Lexie to more danger for that, and he also wouldn't leave her alone. Which meant he'd have to wait for his dad or Matt to stop by for dinner before taking care of business.

He pulled up to the house and spotted Ruth's ranch hand stepping down from his truck, the horse trailer hitched behind.

Gavin shifted into Park. "What's Jose doing here?"

"Taking Misty home." Lexie unbuckled her seat belt.

"With you staying on the property, there's no point in moving her, is there?"

She firmed her jaw. "I can't impose on your family to care for her or pay for her feed."

"As Dad said, you're practically—"

"I'm not family, and I never will be," Lexie snapped.

Her bitter tone cut him to the quick, but he wouldn't ignore her barb again.

"My family loves you, Lex," he said, careful not to say he loved her, too, though he did and always would, he supposed. He just wasn't sure if he was still *in* love with her. "They're happy to help you out."

"And I appreciate it, I really do, but…" She drew in a long breath. "But being with them when we're no longer a couple is awkward."

He swiveled to get a better read on her emotions. "You seemed right at home with them, so I never considered that."

"I am at home here, and I like being with them. All of them. But…" She shook her head.

"But what, sug—" Her fiery gaze at his almost slip had him physically pulling back, but he wouldn't let this drop. "But what?"

"But spending time with them only to have you leave again will make it harder for me."

"Another thing I didn't think of." He resisted sighing, as this wasn't about him. "I'm such a dolt."

She peered at him and her lips started turning up in a grin. "For an FBI agent, you do miss the obvious sometimes."

He should smile with her but he couldn't. "I don't miss a thing on the job, but I have to admit, I haven't been as in tune with you as I should be."

"Why do you think that is?" she asked softly.

"Honestly?" He paused for a second. "Because I don't know how I feel about you and I've been trying to avoid thinking about it."

"Me, too," she admitted. "And I think it's a good idea

that we keep on avoiding it." She grabbed her door handle. "I'll just help Jose get Misty loaded up."

"I wish you'd reconsider."

"I'm already imposing. I won't be a financial burden, too." She opened her door. "Once Misty is on the road, I'll help you carry in boxes."

She jumped down and crossed the driveway. For a moment, Gavin watched her go. Her thick head of hair, gathered into a high ponytail, swished as she walked. She wore her little red boots and dressier jeans, along with the same parka from last night. The big hood seemed to dwarf her, adding to her look of vulnerability.

Tessa stepped outside and waved when she spotted them. She'd gotten in late last night and was out of the house by the time he'd come down for breakfast, so he hadn't seen his sister yet. Eager to talk to her, he headed for the stables.

She opened the gate and stood back. A fiery redhead, she took after their nana and was the only sibling without dark hair. They'd often teased her growing up that she was adopted among other things and still did. She'd balked as a kid, but took it all in stride now and gave as good as she got.

"I'm sorry for your loss, Lexie," she said, her eyes, more russet than the McKade deep brown, filled with sadness.

"Thank you." Lexie smiled a soft, sweet number that Gavin wished she'd offer him. "It's good to see you."

"You, too. We should have kept in touch better."

Tessa closed the gate behind them, then launched herself at Gavin and gave him a fierce hug. Regret tugged at him. He hated what he was doing to his family by staying away. Man, if only he could change it.

"Wish you'd get it in your stubborn head to leave those Feds and come home where you belong," she whispered.

She smelled of her familiar scent of lab chemicals mixed with horse. A huge tomboy, growing up, she competed in rodeo barrel racing and could rarely be found with her boots on the ground instead of in stirrups. Somewhere around high school, she discovered boys and found her feminine side. Still, she wasn't afraid to get dirty on a crime scene and was more at home in boots and jeans than heels and a skirt.

He pulled back. "Anything new on any of the crime scenes?"

"Still waiting on the ATF to give us something of value, and the other scenes are a bust." She sighed. "So you're going to be working with Dad on this, huh?"

He nodded.

"Does that mean maybe you can see your way to work with him again on a full-time basis?"

"It's way too early in my visit to go there, squirt." He ruffled her hair. "I'll just see if Jose needs help getting Misty ready to leave."

"Watch where you step," she said. "Wouldn't want you to mess up those fancy shoes."

"Careful, squirt." Gavin planted his arm around her shoulders and rubbed his knuckles over her hair. "You're still the smallest one in the family, and I can easily still wrestle you to the ground. You wouldn't want to get your pretty red hair dirty."

"You two never change." Lexie chuckled before a wistful look settled on her face.

"Let's get Misty on the trailer," he said to move them forward and away from dwelling on all that she'd lost out on.

In the stable, he breathed deep of the hay, feeling like

he'd come home again. Tessa squirmed out from under his arm. She was a handful to hold on to, all muscle and little padding. Lexie, on the other hand, was soft and sweet and oh, so wonderful to hold.

He dragged his gaze away from her and from the corner of his eye caught Tessa watching him. She pushed boundaries in much the same way he did, but she didn't have the added burden of being the oldest sibling. Before this trip was over, he suspected he'd get an earful from her on why he shouldn't have left Lexie behind.

Manners had him wanting to take over Lexie's work, but he knew she loved caring for Misty, so he stood back and said nothing until Jose was heading down the drive with the trailer.

Gavin tipped his head at his vehicle. "After I unload the boxes, I have some paperwork to catch up on. You can either stay at the main house with me, or I'll grab my things and come to the cabin."

"Main house is fine," she quickly said when she looked like she really wanted to say neither.

At his vehicle, Gavin grabbed the first few boxes, stacking them in his father's office. He made another trip and Lexie helped carry in the boxes. Once upon a time, they would be laughing and cutting up, but now tension lingered between them, making the job seem like it took longer to complete.

Finally, she dropped the last box in place. "I'll go see if your mom or nana need help making lunch."

"Thank you, Lex," he said. "I know they both like having you here."

He caught her frown before she left the room. No matter what he said, it was the wrong thing, and he needed to get used to that. He shook it off and removed the disgruntled patients' files. To spread out on the desk, he moved the glass appreciation plaque given to his dad after twenty-five years of service to the county. Gavin remembered the award ceremony and how he'd thought at the time that he would receive such a plaque some-day, too. Wishful thinking and no point indulging in it.

He laid out his files then opened his laptop, where he called up a database of patients for nearby clinics sus-pected of Medicaid fraud. He entered Silas Ross's name and clicked Search.

The Lowell Clinic in Cumberland had recently added Ross's name, just as Helen had mentioned. His search of Billy Howard and Rex Sanderson produced the same results. For kicks, he entered Earl Clark and both of the Nash men's names, but they didn't return any records. He didn't know what to make of his findings at this point other than those three patients had moved on to the near-est clinic.

He plugged each name into law-enforcement data-bases and learned that Sanderson had prior arrests for drug possession and confirmed Ross's record, too. How-ard was clean.

Given a choice, Gavin would go with the men with priors, and of the two of them, Gavin knew Ross pos-sessed the skills to detonate the plane. He flipped to Ross's patient file and tried to read Dr. Grant's notes, but he couldn't decipher the handwriting. Same was true of Sanderson and Howard.

Maybe Lexie could read the chicken scratching. He grabbed the files and found Lexie with his mom and nana in the kitchen. Lexie wore his nana's apron, her hands covered in flour as she cut out biscuits. She was humming until he stepped into the room and her frown returned.

Was she ever going to forgive him? Probably not until he got her to see things from his point of view, which she'd never done. But then, had he really taken the time to try to understand what she was feeling or had he needed to escape so badly that he'd focused only on himself?

"Did you need something?" She wiped the flour-covered back of her hand across her forehead, leaving behind a white trail that he wanted to brush away.

Instead, he held out the top folder. "I'm hoping you can decipher your dad's handwriting and help me figure out why these patients were seeing him."

She went to the sink to wash her hands then sat at the small table and scanned the folders. "Looks like they were all pain management clients, and Dad prescribed narcotics." She stabbed a finger at a few of the notes. "See? Here and here?"

He peered at the files. "And does their reason for moving on to a new doctor match with Helen's statement?"

She nodded. "He refused to prescribe additional meds and they left. She didn't mention narcotics, though. Do you think my dad was writing too many narcotic prescriptions and his death is somehow related to that?"

Gavin shook his head. "We checked that out already. He's not on the DEA's radar for writing excessive scripts. So, no, I don't think it has to do with prescriptions he generated."

"But you mentioned drugs as a good motive earlier."

"I did, and I'm not ruling out his death being related to drugs. Just not the prescriptions he wrote."

She furrowed her brow. "But what else could there be?"

"I don't know at this point," he admitted. "But locating these men so I can talk to them could very well help us figure that out. I have a last known address for all three of them and that's a good place to start."

She stood and turned to his grandmother. "Mind if I bail on the biscuits so I can help Gavin?"

His nana waved her hand. "Go on now. I like seeing you two together and not at odds with each other."

"Mom." His mother's tone warned his nana not to go there, but Gavin could see his mother shared the sentiment.

Honestly, he liked not being at odds with Lexie, as well. Liked it too much for his own good, so as he headed for the office where they'd be alone together, he warned himself to keep things professional.

He took a seat behind his father's big desk and Lexie came to stand behind him. Her sweet scent caught his attention and it was all he could do to remember his thoughts of a moment ago to remain professional. He forced his attention to the computer and entered the patients' names into the DMV database. The search returned the same addresses.

"They all live in apartments in various cities in the county. Silas resides here in Lost Creek, but Matt mentioned he may have moved. I'll give the apartment managers a call to see if they're all still at the same addresses."

As he picked up his phone, Lexie went to stare out the window. He had to admit to being thankful that she'd chosen to put some distance between them, making it easier to concentrate on his calls. It was all he could do not to stare at her framed in the sunlight and make his calls.

When he'd finished talking to the managers, he swiveled to look at her. "They've all moved on. No forwarding address."

She turned. "Don't you find that odd?"

"I do for Silas, as he's older and he was holding down a steady job. But people who live in apartments are more mobile, and if they have any issues with the law, they often take off without forwarding addresses."

"So now what?" she asked.

"Now we move on to Facebook."

She snorted. "What? Like they'll brag about being involved in drugs on Facebook?"

"You'd be surprised. Criminals aren't often the brightest, so it may sound far-fetched, but many cases are solved when they brag on social media. But even if they don't, you can often locate people just by reading through their posts."

Since Silas was the only one of the three on both lists, he entered Silas's name and his profile came up. In his picture, he had a crooked smirk and his hair hung in eyes that were glassy, leading Gavin to think Silas used drugs.

Gavin clicked on his picture to enlarge it. "Is he of the right build to be the biker?"

She leaned closer. "Could be."

Gavin pointed out for Lexie that Silas's About page had listed him living in Cumberland.

"Let's look at his feed to see if there are any pictures of the complex where he lives." Gavin read down the posts, mostly about beer brewing, but one item caught his attention.

"Look at this." He pointed to the screen update and read, "'Lowell Clinic rocks. 'Bout time I found a decent doctor. If he shows up on time tomorrow afternoon.'"

"He has an appointment tomorrow." Lexie's voice rose with excitement and her eyes gleamed.

"See? Social media helps in many ways." Gavin smiled up at her and got caught up in her beauty.

"You can catch him when he goes to the appointment. And thanks to Facebook, you'll have no trouble recognizing him." She suddenly threw her arms around his neck and hugged him.

Her touch caught him off guard but it felt so right that he came to his feet and pulled her closer. Surprisingly, she didn't push him away but settled her head on his chest. Holding her was just like he remembered, and he wanted more. So much more. Starting with a kiss.

He pulled back, and as he lowered his head, she shoved him away.

"I'm sorry," she said, looking shocked by her actions. "I should never have done that. I don't know what got into me. It doesn't mean anything, though. I was just so happy to have a lead, and you were...well...convenient, so I... Anyway, it's good news about the lead."

Right, the lead. He had an investigation to solve. A career to advance, a killer to find, and he should be equally happy. Then why was his heart aching and his stomach tied up in knots?

TEN

Walt had just finished the lemon chicken and red potatoes Winnie had kept warm for him after a big accident caused by an unexpected snowfall had kept him from getting home on time for dinner.

Due to their higher elevation, they often got a light snowfall each winter and Adam was outside playing in the fluffy powder. Lexie wanted to join him, but she didn't want to miss the update from today's investigation, which Walt declared he'd reveal from his recliner in the family room.

Matt, Jed and Gavin were already seated in the cozy room when she stepped under the large archway. A fresh scent wafted from the cinnamon-infused pinecones on the fireplace mantel above a roaring fire, and her gaze landed on the Christmas stockings quilted by Betty. Lexie couldn't resist running her fingers over Gavin's embroidered name. She looked up to find him watching her as he'd been doing a lot today. She dropped her hand and focused on Walt before he came over to join her.

"I talked to Norbert and Freddie Nash today." Walt lifted the recliner handle on his chair. "They both have alibis. Course, I'm not taking their word for it, and I've got Kendall running down the alibis right now."

"Anything in any of the interviews to suggest our suspects partnered with the doc or have a grudge against him?" Gavin asked.

"Not so far. Earl Clark wasn't at home or answering his phone. Checked a couple of times. Then I called the garage and Clem told me Earl works tomorrow. So I plan to pop in on him unannounced in the morning."

"I'll go with you," Gavin said.

Walt raised his brow, and Lexie wasn't surprised to see father and son duke it out without saying a word.

"Wouldn't two investigators be better than one?" she said before Walt said no. "You might pick up on something the other one misses."

"Good point," Walt conceded. "But I'm taking lead."

"No problem," Gavin replied. "Someone will need to stay with Lexie while we go."

"I can spare Dylan for the morning, but need him on patrol by noon."

Gavin gave a quick nod and explained what they learned from Facebook about Silas Ross. "He's Dr. Grant's former patient."

"Facebook," Walt scoffed. "You can't believe what you read on there. His DMV records still have him listed in Lost Creek."

Lexie waited for Gavin to dispute his father's claim about Facebook, but he simply blew out a breath. "I called the manager for Silas's last known address. He's moved on."

"No wonder we haven't seen him in town," Matt said. "But even if it takes an hour to get to Cumberland from here, it seems kind of drastic to move just because he changed doctors."

"His company is up that way, too, right?" Jed said. "So that would make more sense."

Gavin nodded. "Whatever the reason for his move, he posted on Facebook that he has a doctor's appointment in the afternoon, so I'll stake the place out."

"Sounds like a good plan," Matt said.

Walt frowned but didn't say anything else.

"So if that's it…" Matt stretched. "I haven't slept in over twenty-four hours and I need some shut-eye."

"Lightweight," Gavin joked. "Going to bed and it's not even seven."

"Give it a rest," Walt said. "He works hard and needs to sleep."

"I get it, Dad. I was just razzing him."

Lexie cringed at Gavin's sharp tone and waited for Walt to respond.

"That's okay, Dad." Matt winked and punched Gavin in the arm on the way past. "We all know the Feds are slackers."

The brothers laughed.

At one time Lexie would have joined in, but felt like laughing now would send the message that she'd forgiven Gavin when she wasn't anywhere near doing so.

She heard the door open. Assuming it was Adam, she went to the foyer. He closed the door and stomped the snow from his boots. His cheeks were apple red and he wore a cute grin she hadn't seen in years.

"Looks like you had fun," she said.

He shed his boots and jacket in a pile on the rug then started to step away.

"Um, hello," Lexie said and pointed at his clothing on the rug.

He turned, the smile gone, and an exaggerated sigh slipped from his mouth as he hung up his jacket and set his boots off to the side. Then his phone came out and he headed under another archway into the dining room, where his schoolbooks awaited him.

Though the house had separate rooms, the wide openings made it feel like one big space and Lexie could hear Gavin and Walt arguing.

She was too hyped up to join them, and they didn't need a witness to their discord, so she stayed in the entry and prowled around the space, pacing past the big arches a few times. She finally stepped up to the tree and fingered a few ornaments as she heard the argument end.

"I hate to see you this way," Gavin said from behind her.

Startled, she spun. "What way?"

"Unsettled. Nervous. I understand it, but you have to know you're safe with us."

With the way he'd been trying to ignore her, she kept forgetting how well he knew her and could read her nonverbal signals if he wanted to. "I know but…"

"Why don't we go on a trail ride? That always relaxes you and it'll be beautiful with the fresh snow."

Yeah, he knew her, all right. Whenever life got her down, she'd turned to Misty. Too bad she'd insisted Misty be taken home.

"You can ride Beauty," he said, preempting her first line of defense.

"You don't think Kendall would mind?"

"She won't. But if you'd like, I can text her to ask."

"That would be great. But only if you think it's safe."

"The killer would be a fool to come here with all the law-enforcement officers in place." Gavin smiled, one of those crooked boyish ones that always got to her. "And if it'll make you feel better, we'll only ride up to the pond."

The thought of the pond with snow covering the ground,

the skies clear now and the moon shining off the crystals, cinched her agreement. "Text Kendall."

He took out his phone and tapped the screen. "I'll change clothes while we wait for her to respond."

Lexie nodded, but her mind had already gone to the upcoming ride. They'd be together. Just the two of them. Heading for the spot where she'd once expected he'd propose under a starlit night. Maybe the ride wasn't such a good idea. She'd invite Adam, but he didn't need to be around Gavin. Plus her brother wasn't much of a horseman. Despite how often she or Ruth had tried to coax him onto a horse, he'd rather sit in the house with a computer or his phone in front of him.

Winnie entered the foyer.

"Gavin and I are going for a ride up to the pond," Lexie said, as she thought someone should know they'd gone out riding.

"Perfect night for it with the fresh snow." Winnie's eyes twinkled.

Her attempt at matchmaking was far from subtle.

Walt joined them, his empty coffee cup in hand. "See that Gavin's mind stays on checking the surroundings and not on how pretty you look under the stars."

Adam's head shot up at that one.

"Do you want to come with us?" she asked her brother.

He shook his head and bent over his phone again. *Grrr.* She needed to help him find an interest other than what he could do with electronics. She appreciated her phone for being able to check email and social media. Catch up on the news. Check the weather. But having it in front of her face nearly every waking moment was beyond her understanding.

She looked at Walt and Winnie. "Do either of you want to ride with us?"

She received a shake of heads. "You don't know what you'll be missing."

"A sore rear end and frostbite, you mean?" Winnie laughed and traded her full mug for Walt's. "Sit, and I'll fill yours for you."

They departed, and Lexie went to Adam. She put a hand on his shoulder so he would look at her.

"I have my phone. Call or text me if you need anything. We should be back in an hour or so."

"I got it. I'm not a baby." He was good at pushing boundaries, but he was rarely rude like this.

"When you're under my roof, Adam—" Walt's voice came from the other room "—you'll respect your elders. Now apologize to your sister."

"I'm sorry," he said, real contrition in his tone.

She squatted next to his chair. "We're all under a lot of stress. I get it and understand that it can make us short-tempered."

"Yeah, well…yeah. Right."

She squeezed his hand. "We can head over to the cabin when I get back, okay?"

He nodded eagerly.

"See you in a bit." She stepped back into the foyer to wait for Gavin and turned her attention to the tree.

She spotted a varnished dough ornament of a pair of snowmen wearing Santa hats. Her name and Gavin's were painted below the snowmen, along with a date four Christmases ago. Winnie had snowmen ornaments with each child's birth date. When Lexie and Gavin had gotten serious, she'd added this one so Lexie had a place on their family tree. Lexie searched and found the one Winnie had gotten for Adam, too. She rested the delicate ornament in her hand, her eyes filling with tears. For the

McKade kindness. For the loss of her mother. The loss of her father. Of Gavin.

Father, why? Why put us through all of this? Are You really not there or do You just not care about Adam and me?

"Ready to go?" Gavin asked.

Lexie jerked. The ornament went flying.

He lurched forward and caught it a foot from the floor.

"You scared me," she said. "I almost... It would have been horrible to break Adam's ornament."

Gavin studied her face. "Everything will be okay."

Not wanting to respond to what she felt was a platitude, she grabbed her jacket from a hook and stepped onto the porch lit by the moon's bright glow. She took a few deep breaths of the sharp air and sighed out her tension. She heard Gavin say goodbye to his parents as she descended the stairs. Snow covered her boots and she stared at it as she waited at the bottom.

She looked up to see him step onto the porch, and her thoughts shifted. He was dressed in worn jeans that fit as if custom made for him. He wore scuffed boots and a denim jacket and had settled his favorite cowboy hat on his head. The sight of him standing before her, looking so ruggedly handsome, pulled at her heartstrings.

And her mind wandered to a place it had no business going.

His formal agent attire had helped her keep her feelings in check, but seeing him like this? Seeing the old Gavin. The Gavin she used to know, and love, was almost more than she could bear.

She whipped around and started for the corral. A moment later, she heard him jogging to keep up.

"I need you to stay closer to me." He shifted the rifle in his arms.

"But you said it was safe."

"Nothing is one hundred percent safe, Lexie. We can never let our guard down."

At the urgency in his tone, she shot him a look. "You've changed."

"What do you mean?" he asked.

"You're always on edge."

"It's the situation."

"No, it's more," she insisted. "Even at Dad's office, you were tightly wound. Like you're expecting something bad to happen at any moment and you have to be on guard for it."

He shrugged. "That's the life of a law-enforcement officer."

"True, but you weren't like this when you were a deputy. Sure, you were cautious and carried all the time… but this? This over-the-top need to control. That's new."

He peered at her as if he wanted to say something but thought better of it and then suddenly grabbed the gate and opened it.

Fine. Be that way. It would be far better on the ride if they kept this wall up between them anyway.

They saddled the horses and Gavin dropped a pair of binoculars in his saddlebag and his rifle into the holder. She knew he was just taking precautions, but still, her nerves were fried, and she really needed to gallop across the field with Beauty. She mounted the horse and urged her into a slow walk. Gavin rode up beside her, and they galloped toward the lake, the crisp air whipping at Lexie's face. Each strike of Beauty's hooves kicked up snow, and Lexie felt like she was in a winter wonderland painting.

She let go of the stress. Let go of the worry. The fear. A killer may be stalking her, but right now, there was nothing but her and Beauty, the wind and the man she was trying so hard to ignore.

By the pond, Gavin watched as Lexie slipped off Beauty and literally pranced through the snow, throwing her arms out in excitement. She spun in a circle then dropped to the ground and swished her arms and legs over the fluffy powder to create a symmetrical angel. "Isn't it breathtaking?"

"Gorgeous," he said and meant it, but he only had eyes for her.

Lexie lay for a moment, her smile wide and warming his heart. She suddenly jumped up like a little child and brushed the snow from her clothes then rushed over to a rock at the edge of the pond. Plopping down, she raised her face to the stars, her contented look making Gavin suck in a breath.

Her smile broadened. "This was such a good idea."

Gavin dismounted and moved closer to her, but there was no way he was sitting down. Not with a killer out there. He kept his gaze roving the area. "It must feel good to catch your breath after dealing with the hordes of McKades."

"You exaggerate. It's not a horde until they all show up." She grinned. "Besides, I love your family. Sunday dinners with them are some of my fondest memories of when we were together."

"Ouch." He faked pulling a knife from his chest.

She tsked. "I'm serious. You've always taken them for granted. I mean, sure, you don't get along with your dad, but for the most part, he's a good father. Not like my fa—" She pressed a hand over her mouth. "I guess it really hasn't hit me that he's gone."

"I'm so sorry, Lexie."

She shook her head as if shaking away her pain. "Besides passing each other on the street, I only saw him a couple of times a year, but you know… I'm… It's…" She pulled her feet up on the rock and rested her chin on her knees. "I think it's the thought that we'll never have a chance to reconcile that's hitting me the hardest. Despite years of being ignored and belittled by him, I always hoped a day would come where we could bury the hatchet and go back to the way we were before Mom died."

She suddenly jumped to her feet and grabbed Gavin's hand, her fingers insistent. "You have to let this serve as a lesson to you. Find a way to get along with your dad. Now. Before it's too late."

"I…" he began, but couldn't even put words to a thought he didn't believe. Sure, she was right. He didn't have forever to patch things up with his dad, but a peace accord had to be a two-way street, and the ornery old guy wasn't likely going to meet him in the middle.

"Just promise me you'll try, okay?" She sought his gaze and held it with a tearful one of her own, resurrecting memories of their time together after run-ins with her dad. Times when Gavin would have done most anything to erase those tears and he was helpless to deny her anything.

"I promise," he said, wondering how in the world he was going to hold to his promise.

They were locked in each other's gazes, tension crackling between them. He didn't even try to come up with a subject, as he figured anything they might discuss would end awkwardly. They'd been in love. Deeply. And yet he'd had to walk away, leaving her hurt and confused.

Maybe he'd been confused, too, as he'd chosen to leave town, and yet, as she stood before him, looking so beautiful and achingly vulnerable, he realized how very much he missed her. He hadn't met another woman who compared to her. Not that he'd been looking. Not with his heart still raw years after their breakup.

But despite the pain, he couldn't move back here. He just couldn't. Being a lawman was in his blood. From generation to generation, and he couldn't bear the thought of doing anything else. Working for his father was the only law-enforcement gig in the area, and that he couldn't abide. So he had to stay away. Even if it meant never being with Lexie.

Gavin scrubbed a hand across his jaw and released a long, frustrated breath. He couldn't stand there in limbo—wanting her and yet knowing he couldn't have her. "Do you want to ride again?"

Looking forlorn now, she nodded, and he boosted her onto Beauty's back. She didn't argue or frown at his assistance, which was a huge improvement over yesterday, as far as he was concerned. He wouldn't put any stock in it, though, as he was sure her sudden compliance stemmed from being distraught over her father.

He got Lightning moving and they meandered along the trail toward the ranch. Taking it slower on the return trip gave him time to look around at the ground covered in a pristine white blanket. Why couldn't he find a way to cover his life this way? To forget his issues with his father and make a fresh start?

Because life didn't work that way, that was why. You couldn't simply lay a blanket over it and—presto—have all your problems solved. It simply hid them for another day, and when that blanket of snow melted, they were still there.

He heard a branch snap in the distance and would have thought he'd imagined the sound except Lightning's head picked up at the noise. Could be related to the snow clinging to the branches, but Gavin wouldn't take any chances.

Grabbing his binoculars and rising up in his stirrups, he scanned the area. At a scenic overlook on a nearby road, he saw movement and stilled Lightning so he could zoom in. He scanned again.

His heart rate kicked up and he dropped into his saddle. "We need to go, now!"

Lexie's eyes widened. "What's wrong?"

"There's a man at the scenic overlook watching us."

ELEVEN

Lexie kicked Beauty faster, the wind biting into her face. Why had she sent Misty home? She knew how to handle and communicate with her. Sure, Beauty was usually a gentle ride, but the sudden change in movement left her unsettled and her hooves pummeled over the ground in wild abandon. The last thing Lexie needed was to fall from the horse. Actually, the last thing she needed was for the man watching them to come after them.

She glanced over her shoulder. No one was chasing them. Had they gone far enough so if this guy fired a gun that a bullet wouldn't reach them? She wasn't familiar with weapons, so she had no idea. Which meant keeping Beauty racing fast.

At the house, Gavin dropped from Lightning before fully stopping. He looped the horse's reins on a rough wooden fence and then jerked Lexie from Beauty's back. Her feet had barely hit the ground when he grabbed her hand and flew toward the steps, pulling her behind him. She tripped on the bottom stair, so he scooped her into his arms and kept moving in one seamless motion.

Terrified or not, the awareness of being in his arms cut through her feelings. He pushed open the door and she wished he'd set her free as much as she wished he'd keep holding her. She longed to be held by him again and the reality was even better than her memories.

He looked deeply into her eyes. "Are you okay?"

"Fine," she replied, though her heart beat as fast as Beauty's hooves had struck the ground.

Gavin scooped her closer. Held her tighter. She circled her arms around his neck. Wanting to kiss him, she lifted her face.

"What's wrong, Lex?" Adam called out from the dining room. He was a teenager, but they were so close that he had the ability to sense her distress.

"Don't worry, bud. I'm fine." She dropped her arms and tried to squirm free.

Gavin held fast and carried her into the family room, where his parents and grandparents were watching television. He gently set her on her feet. She heard Adam follow them into the room.

"There was a man watching us from the overlook," Gavin said. "I'm leaving Lexie here and going after him."

Walt jumped up from his chair. Winnie's eyes narrowed and Betty sat forward.

"Then let's get after him," Walt said.

"Not so fast." Gavin held out a hand. "I've got this. You stay here with Lexie."

His father eyed him. "It's my county, and if anyone does the staying, it'll be you."

Gavin seemed to weigh his decision and finally looked at his grandfather. "You good to watch over Lexie, Granddad?"

"Course I am." Jed came to his feet. "But don't be in such an all-fire hurry that you forget defensive tactics."

"Be careful," Winnie called out, but they were out the door in a flash and Lexie didn't know if they'd even heard her.

Lexie's fear started to abate and her legs felt like rubber. She nearly collapsed but Jed grabbed her elbow. "Whoa, there, little filly."

Winnie rushed over to her. "C'mon, sweetheart. You need to sit down."

The siren on Walt's car sprang to life outside while Winnie helped Lexie to the sofa, where she gratefully sank into the worn plaid cushions.

"I'll get you some water," Betty offered. On her way, she stopped next to Jed, who was staring out the door, his hand planted on his waist. "I know how much you want to go with them, but there's no holster at your side anymore, dear."

"I know that. How I know that." Yearning lingered in his tone as he closed the door and locked it tight. "I'll go up and get my rifle just in case this weasel comes calling."

Lexie heard his quick footfalls on the stairs and was surprised he could still move that fast. These McKade men would remain protecting others as long as they were physically able, and she, for one, was extremely grateful to have them on her side.

"Are you sure you're okay?" Adam's eyebrow rose, looking so much like their father that Lexie felt tears coming on.

She blinked them away. "I'm fine. How's your homework coming?"

"Need to finish math."

"Go ahead and finish up so when Walt and Gavin get back we can head to the cabin."

Usually he'd argue about the homework, but he gave a clipped nod and, after a long look, left the room. Her mama-bear instincts told her to go after him and talk about the incident, but they also told her not to do so when her emotions were so raw.

Winnie clicked off the television. "I'm sure the last thing you want to listen to is an old episode of *Bonanza*."

"Actually, it's comforting to see the four of you still like to watch it. At least there's something that hasn't changed."

Winnie leaned closer. "I have to admit, the show is more Walt and Jed's joy. Betty and I put up with it and let the men pretend they're in the Old West working the Cartwrights' ranch and protecting their community. But please don't tell them."

Lexie laughed. Oh, how she loved this woman. Lexie wanted to fall into her arms and cry. For herself, sure, but mostly for Adam and the danger he could be in. For the loss of Gavin in their lives. For the pain of seeing him again. For losing this family. This beautiful, wonderful family that she'd hoped to become part of.

"Tell me that you and Gavin had a nice ride until this man intruded," Winnie said.

Lexie swallowed down her distress the same way she'd choked down her father's callous behavior for years. "The ride was lovely."

Betty returned with the water and handed the glass to Lexie. "Now drink up and, once you're up to it, you can tell us what happened."

She settled on the sofa next to Lexie, who caught a hint of the rosemary Betty had used on the fresh focaccia bread she'd made to go with the lemon chicken for dinner.

Lexie drank the water and took a few breaths before telling the women about the night. Not the intimate time at the pond or how she'd felt being with Gavin again, but about their mad dash across the property.

"The horses." She jumped up. "I need to take care of them after such a hard run."

"I don't think it's a good idea to go outside."

Jed poked his head into the room. "This guy has likely skedaddled. Especially after hearing Walt's sirens."

"Still, I don't think Walt or Gavin would appreciate Lexie going outside," Winnie said. "I can take care of the horses."

Lexie shook her head. "Working with them will help me calm down."

"But—"

"I'll go out with her," Jed interrupted, lifting his rifle. "She'll be fine."

Winnie opened her mouth to say something, but Lexie marched to the door before she continued to argue. Still, Lexie wasn't foolhardy, so she waited for Jed to join her on the porch before descending the stairs and taking Beauty's reins from the fence rail. She approached Lightning with caution, letting him smell her before touching his nose. He whinnied his acceptance, and she was glad he remembered her and would let her lead him to the stable.

Jed crossed his rifle over his chest while letting his gaze rove the area as they walked. "You've had quite a few days of it, haven't you?"

She nodded. "I'm thankful for your family's support."

"It's nothing. Only wish I was out there with the others tracking this guy."

"I'm glad you're here, or I'd be stuck inside instead of spending time with the horses." She opened the corral gate and led the horses into the stable.

"I'd help out, but it's best for me to stand watch at the door."

"No worries." Lexie moved deeper into the stable.

She should walk the horses after the hard run, but Jed wouldn't allow her to spend time outside. The walking would have to wait for the men, if they got back before the horses cooled off.

She started the grooming process by loosening the girth then removing the bridle and replacing it with a halter and lead shank for each horse. She would have to rinse off the bits, wipe off sweat and dirt from the saddle and girth and put the tack away, but first she wanted to give the horses water, so she led them to the trough.

Lexie stroked Beauty's nose before she dipped it into the cool water. "Thank you for bringing me safely home, girl."

"You and Tessa are a lot alike," Jed called out. "Give her a horse to talk to and she's happy as a lark."

Lexie couldn't disagree. Misty had been with her for years. Her companion, allowing her to unload all her feelings after Gavin left. She wanted to unload now, too, but not with Jed within hearing distance, so she waited until Beauty drank her fill then rested her head against Beauty's neck and stroked her soft head. She loved the feel of her, and how she simply stood and let Lexie absorb comfort.

As much as Lexie wanted to stand there, she needed to examine the horses for any problems from the ride. By the time she'd checked for rubs and chafing from the saddle and tack, and the legs for cuts, bumps and bruises, she heard a car rumbling up the driveway.

"The men are back," Jed said. "I'll tell Gavin you're here."

Lexie nodded, but she was afraid to hear what he'd discovered.

Jed yelled to Gavin and then she heard a single set

of footsteps. She looked out the window to see Gavin headed their way and Walt marching up to the house.

Gavin crossed over to her. "You don't have to take care of the horses. I can do it."

"I'm glad to. Besides, it took my mind off the man."

"Any luck?" Jed asked.

"He was long gone by the time we got there," Gavin said disgustedly. "But Dad called Tessa to the overlook, and she may have found a lead."

"A good one?" Jed asked.

Gavin shrugged. "She lifted an oily footprint and another substance she couldn't identify from where the car was parked. The oil appears fresh. It might mean nothing, but it could also tie the mechanic we'll be questioning in the morning to the scene. She collected samples and will send them to the nearest lab for processing."

"How long does evidence processing like this take nowadays?" Jed asked.

"Depending on the lab's priorities and backlog, it could be days—even weeks—but Dad will use his influence to get the tests moved up the calendar. Still, it will most likely take three days or so before we hear anything."

"Three days," Lexie muttered and hoped that it wouldn't be that long because with Gavin standing close, his scent firing her senses, she didn't know how long she could continue to keep him at arm's length.

Gavin stood by the fireplace, presumably to warm his hands, but Lexie's warning to reconcile with his dad before it was too late continued to plague him. His gaze went to his father as he sat in his big leather chair and talked to Lexie. Her respect for him was evident in her look. A respect Gavin had once been blessed to have.

He glanced at his parents and grandparents. Such a

strong family unit that he'd once thought couldn't be cracked. Until he'd taken off and left behind a wide fissure. He missed each of them for different reasons. His mom and nana for their unreserved love. His granddad for companionship. No one made a better fishing buddy. His dad—for what? An admirable role model to emulate most of the time, as well as a strong leader of his family and men. All of them for the way they let their faith guide them. Something he'd completely ignored for years.

He needed to admit it once and for all. He wanted to come back here. But it wasn't possible. Not with his father's reaction when he'd learned of the man at the lookout. His dad had jumped up to take charge, claiming territory and barreling over Gavin's plan. Gavin's gut had cried out to take lead so nothing could go wrong, and it had been on the tip of his tongue to tell his dad to back off. But it wasn't just his dad he would have fended off. Shockingly, since Emily had been shot, he didn't trust anyone to help him. Not even a family member.

Lexie stood. "It's a school night, and I need to get Adam over to the cabin."

Gavin crossed his arms and widened his stance in preparation for the battle he knew was coming. "I'm staying at the cabin with you and Adam."

She lifted her chin. "No."

As much as he hated arguing with her, he found her stance cute and nearly irresistible. "It's nonnegotiable."

"It's a solid plan," Walt said.

She opened her mouth, likely to argue, when Adam joined them. "I think Gavin should stay with us, too."

Lexie's mouth dropped open. Gavin's almost did, too. With Adam so mad, asking Gavin to stay at the cabin meant he had to be seriously afraid.

"Okay, then." Lexie gave in, sounding defeated in more ways than one.

Gavin had to ignore her pain and move on before she changed her mind. "Give me a minute to grab a few things."

He gathered only a couple of items he'd need for the night from his room, as he planned to come back here to shower and change in the morning. He picked up his computer and a few files, and hurried to escort the pair down the stairs and into the snow.

Adam held out a hand. "I'll carry your bag for you."

Gavin didn't need the help, but he saw the offer for what was intended and handed over the bag. "Thanks, man. Mind helping me keep an eye out as we walk over there?"

Adam nodded and shouldered the bag. Gavin turned to discover Lexie watching them. He couldn't read her eyes in the shadowed night, but he hoped she would be happy that Adam was feeling less hostile toward him.

They walked in silence, their footfalls barely audible in the snow. They passed six small cabins, a fire pit blazing with a roaring fire and ringed by wide stumps where several guests roasted marshmallows. Another couple tossed snowballs and shrieked as they ran from them. The kind of picture-perfect scene that would make a great advertisement for the dude ranch.

He unlocked the largest cabin's door, ushered the pair inside, then checked every inch of the four-room building. "You two go ahead and get settled while I step out to talk to the guests by the campfire in case they saw anything odd tonight."

Lexie paused in taking off her jacket. "But the trail is nowhere near here."

"True, but I won't leave any possible lead unexplored."

"Keep an eye on her while I'm gone, okay?" he said to Adam as he passed.

Adam nodded, and Gavin was thankful that, for now, the teen didn't cast a hateful look his way.

Gavin stepped up to the roaring fire. Two men and one woman looked up. One man sat off to the side, and Gavin knew from looking at the guest list that he was alone and the other two were a couple, as was the pair frolicking in the snow.

"Evening," Gavin said. "Mind if I join you?"

"Please," the single guy said.

Gavin gave his first name and learned this guy was Dean, the woman Anita, and her husband, Randy. All names matched the guest register.

"You staying at the big cabin?" Dean asked.

"Just settling in." Gavin took a seat on the far side of the fire to keep cabin in view. "Nice night even if it's cold and snowy."

"That's what the fire is for." Dean chuckled.

"With that pile of red-hot embers, it looks like you all have been out here for a while."

"Started the fire right at sundown."

"What about the other guests?" Gavin asked, though he knew that, other than the couple in the snow, no other guests were registered. "Any of them join you?"

"What others?" Randy laughed. "Not too many people foolish enough to rough it in the cold like this and right before Christmas."

"Really, no other guests?" Gavin asked. "I thought I saw a guy hanging out at the overlook a couple of hours ago."

"Now, that's just plain nuts," Anita said. "It would be

crazy cold without a fire." She slid her arm around Randy's shoulders. "Or love to keep you warm."

She laughed, and Randy joined in, but Dean looked like he might be sick.

Gavin moved on, mixing small talk with tossed-out questions he thought they'd find innocuous. It soon became clear that they hadn't seen anything, so he excused himself and returned to the cabin. On the way, he received a text update from his father.

Inside, he found Lexie sitting on the sofa and a light spilling out from the bedroom where Adam poked his head out. Gavin exchanged a nod with the boy telling him everything was okay, and he stepped back into his room. Gavin took a seat next to Lexie, careful to put a safe zone between them.

"I've been thinking about the car you saw," she said. "Can't you track it?"

"All I caught was that it was a small Honda. Likely an Accord, which is too common of a make and model to begin searching by that criteria alone. And Dad just texted to say none of the men on our suspect list own a Honda."

"Maybe it's the mechanic, and he borrowed one of the cars in for repair."

"I'll ask him about it in the morning." He pointed to her tablet. "What are you up to?"

"Returning an email from the funeral home. They told me that the ME hasn't released Dad's body yet."

"That's not unusual in a murder investigation."

"Just hearing you say that dumbfounds me." She sighed. "I mean, how did my life come to this? To a murder investigation, the loss of my father. Much less having someone trying to abduct me and ransack my home and truck."

"I know it's a shock, Lex. To me, too. Especially around here. You know if I could change things for you, I would."

She nodded but didn't speak.

"Have you thought any more about talking to your dad's lawyer?"

"I've thought about it, but I still don't see the point."

He leaned toward her and captured her gaze. "What if he left money for Adam? Won't be long before he goes to college and could need the money."

"I've set aside enough money for him," she insisted.

"That's good but—"

She held up a hand. "I don't want to talk about it, Gavin. Not now. Not ever. So promise you won't bring it up again."

"See, here's the thing," he said, wishing he could just let it alone, but he felt a deep-seated need to speak. "You want me to reconcile with my dad, but even in death you haven't reconciled with yours."

She snapped back. "It's not the same."

"Isn't it?"

She jumped up and glared at him. "Maybe it is, but I said I don't want to talk about it. Especially not with you. And I mean it." She marched into the other bedroom and closed the door with great force.

After her intensity at the pond, begging him to fix things with his dad, this was the last response he expected from her. But with such a visceral reaction on her part, he'd honor her wishes in this matter going forward.

Well, unless it conflicted with the investigation. Then he'd have to do what he thought best. Even if it pushed an even bigger wedge between them.

TWELVE

As the morning sun climbed into the sky and sparkled off the snow, Gavin wasn't sure if he could bring himself to walk out of the house and leave Lexie behind. She sat at the small kitchen table with Adam, his mother and Matt, and it was easy to see she was still shaken up from last night.

"We don't have all day, Gavin." His dad's voice rang from the foyer.

"You probably don't want to keep Dad waiting," Matt said.

Gavin met his brother's gaze. "You'll call me if the slightest thing happens, or if you hear anything from Kendall at the school."

"Do you think something will happen to Adam?" Lexie's worried expression tugged at him to stay. But he knew she was safe with Matt and Granddad, and Gavin could gain valuable intel by going to the interview.

He smiled for Lexie's sake. "Adam will be fine. I'm just being cautious."

"Something you've become in spades," Matt muttered, drawing Lexie and his mother's attention.

But Gavin ignored his brother's comment and kept his

focus on Lexie. "If anything seems out of the ordinary, you call me, too."

She nodded, but her expression said she was unlikely to turn to him unless the situation was dire. After the way they'd left things last night, he wasn't surprised at her response, but her unwillingness to rely on him still stung.

"Especially if the burner phone rings," he added.

She nodded again and gave him a pointed look that he took to mean she didn't want to discuss that phone in front of Adam.

"Last chance, Gavin," his father bellowed.

Gritting his teeth, he headed for the door only to discover his father had already gone outside and was settling into his car. The moment Gavin hit the passenger seat, his dad shoved the gear into Drive and took off.

Just like last night, his father didn't give a care about Gavin's thoughts or his feelings. Not that his dad would even admit to having feelings. Okay, fine, Gavin might not admit to them much, either, but that wasn't the point. The point was that his dad clearly hadn't changed, and it didn't bode well for their time together.

He merged onto the road. "I called the lab. They're moving the evidence up, but don't hold your breath." He shook his head. "When I first started out in law enforcement, we didn't depend on forensic evaluation as much. But then, we didn't have the levels of crime that we have today."

That piqued Gavin's interest. "The crime rate going up in Lake County?"

"I hate to admit it, but yeah. We've seen an influx of people from the city, and not all of them are law-abiding. So I don't know the people the way I used to. Means I have to depend on forensics more to solve even the smallest of cases."

Surprised at his stance, Gavin peered at his father. "Thought you didn't much like depending on something you couldn't explain."

"That was shortsighted." He glanced at Gavin. "I might be getting old, but I can still change."

Gavin gaped at his father, but he'd already turned his focus back to the road. While the miles disappeared beneath them, Gavin sat back to think. A spark of hope that his father may have changed in other areas took purchase, but he quickly tamped it down. Despite Lexie's valid points about reconciling, it took two people to repair the damage and that meant Gavin had to change, as well, if he wanted to get along with his dad and trust him to have his best interest at heart again.

Was he letting the constant worry from Emily's near death extend to places it shouldn't, like to his siblings? He'd once fully trusted them and happily worked alongside them. But looking back on the last few days, he'd really given them a run for the money. Especially Matt, who was fully competent.

It was one thing not to trust outsiders, but his brother and sisters? He'd sunk way low if he couldn't work with them. He may not be able to do anything else, but that he *could* change. If it extended to his father, then that would be a bonus, and maybe it would help him at work, too.

They hit the outskirts of Lost Creek and his dad pulled into Clem's Garage, with its two gas pumps, an old wrecker and an equally old whitewashed building with a rusty metal awning. The snow was the only fresh-looking thing on the property.

Hoping to see the Honda, Gavin got out to look around, but found only a pickup and minivan parked in the spaces reserved for repair service.

"I'll take lead," his dad called out as he passed Gavin.

He thought to argue, but his promise to try to reconcile came to mind and he bit his tongue.

His dad looked back and arched his bushy eyebrow. "What? No response?"

"Nope." Gavin trailed his dumbfounded father into the shop. The small, grease-stained waiting area was empty, so they pushed through the swinging doors to the repair area holding two bays.

Earl Clark wore dirty denim coveralls that hung on his body. He looked up and ran the back of his hand over a scraggly beard, leaving an oil stain on his cheek.

"Sheriff." Earl switched his focus to Gavin. "Oh, looky what we have here. Heard you come back home… Mr. Big Shot FBI Agent all dressed up in a suit."

Gavin left the guy's barb alone, as it served no purpose in responding.

"You here to harass me like you used to do when you was a deputy?"

"Guess we don't remember things the same way," Gavin said. "You were chopping up hot cars for parts and I was just doing my job."

"*Allegedly* hot cars." Earl crossed his arms. "Never proved that, now, did you?"

"That's water under the bridge," Gavin's father said and Gavin stood back to let his dad do his thing. "I was hoping you could tell us where you were last night around nine."

"Home. Watching TV."

"Can anyone vouch for that?"

"Maybe you should tell me why I need vouching for."

"What about two nights ago? Where were you about the same time and the next morning?"

"That's when that plane exploded and Doc was killed, right?" Earl pulled off a stained Texas Rangers ball cap worn backward and ran a hand through his thinning hair. "You think I had something to do with his death. Unbelievable."

"Clem said you called in sick the next morning."

"That don't mean I killed someone."

"No, it doesn't, but you do have the skills to build a bomb."

A sly grin crossed his mouth. "I do at that. But again, doesn't mean I did it."

"Just tell us where you were," Gavin snapped.

Earl smirked.

"Don't make me haul you in for formal questioning, Earl," Gavin's dad warned.

Gavin hated that his father was keeping his cool when he'd lost it. And he hated that this conversation was going nowhere, so he pulled out his phone and faked checking a text, but turned it on to record Earl's voice for Lexie. Sure, if he confessed to something, the audio wouldn't hold up in court, but Gavin didn't plan to use it in an official capacity.

"Fine," Earl grumbled. "If you must know…it was payday, and I tied one on the night before and was sleeping it off. Again. I was alone."

"Might you have a Honda that you're working on?"

"Not at the moment, no."

"You have one here recently?" Gavin asked.

Earl shrugged.

"If you can't be more specific, I'd like to take a look at your records," Gavin said.

"And I'd like a million bucks." Earl grinned.

"We can get a warrant," Gavin's father said. "Or just ask Clem for the files."

"Clem's not about to give up the records any more than I am."

"Are you sure about that?" Gavin asked. "He willingly told us you called in sick."

A buzzer chimed from the reception area.

"Gotta see to this customer. What with Clem being mad at me for calling in sick an' all, don't want to peeve him off more." That sly grin returned as he walked away.

Gavin followed him and had to fight the urge not to make some smart-alecky comment. It likely wouldn't faze Earl, and if Gavin spouted off in front of a customer, it could only serve to hurt Clem's business.

"That didn't go so well," Gavin said after settling back in the patrol car.

"You liking him for this?" his dad asked.

"He doesn't have a verifiable alibi. He fits the size and build of Lexie's almost abductor, too. So I won't rule him out."

"Agreed, but none of that's enough for me to arrest him." His dad shoved the key into the ignition. "Plus we don't have any obvious motive."

"From what I know about Earl, he doesn't really need a motive to break the law, but killing Dr. Grant and the near abduction took some planning."

"And Earl isn't real big on the planning skills," his father finished for him.

For once Gavin agreed with his dad when he wished he didn't. Because that meant they weren't any closer to finding a suspect and, in his opinion, time was just ticking down until the killer ramped up his efforts to find the information he obviously thought Lexie possessed.

From her spot on the sofa, Lexie heard the front door close and Gavin in the hallway talking with his father. They stepped into the room, both of their gazes tight.

She didn't know if it was because they'd struck out or because they hadn't gotten along.

Gavin marched straight over to her and held out his phone. "I recorded Earl's voice for you. Take a listen and let us know if he's the guy at the airport."

She held her breath as he tapped his screen to get the audio going. Despite her desire to see the killer caught, she was relieved when the man's voice wasn't familiar. "It's not him."

"We didn't think so," Gavin said.

She opened her mouth to respond when the burner phone in her pocket rang. She jumped. "It's the phone from my truck."

"Answer and let me listen in." Gavin sat next to her and, once she lifted the phone to her ear, leaned so close she nearly fumbled the phone.

"Hello?" she answered breathlessly.

"Who is this?" the scrambled voice asked.

"Lexie Grant. Who is this?" she demanded.

Gavin shot her a look that said to cool it.

"You will leave the files in Lost Creek Park," the voice said.

"I don't have any files. You took them."

"Took them? I have no idea what you're talking about, lady. I've looked everywhere. Found nothing. You must have them."

Why was he playing dumb?

"I don't have a clue what information you're looking for," she said.

"Fine. Lie to me. It doesn't matter. You'll bring the files to the park at eleven o'clock. Come alone. No cops. Drop them in the garbage bin at the bench by the swing set. Then leave. I'll be watching. If you don't do what I say, you'll die."

"But I—" she started to say when the call disconnected. She dropped the phone like a burning log on the couch.

Gavin grabbed it and tapped the screen a few times. "We can get records for the caller's phone number, but I imagine it'll lead to another burner phone."

"Trace?" his father asked.

"Call was too short."

Walt widened his stance. "Then we need to do as he says and set up a dummy file for the drop."

Gavin eyed his father. "Lexie's not going anywhere near the park."

"We'll scout it out and go in plain clothes to protect her."

"The caller sounds familiar with the town and could recognize all of us." Gavin scowled at his father. "Even your other deputies."

"Then I'll get deputies from Cypress County."

Gavin jumped up and puffed out his chest as he crossed over to Walt. "They can't protect her from a gunshot."

The sheriff took a matching stance. "She can wear a vest under her jacket."

"And her head?"

"A ballistic helmet under the hood."

"No," Gavin said, his hands curling in fists. "She's not going."

"Listen, son. We need her to do this."

"Will you two stop it," Lexie blurted out. "This is my decision to make."

They both turned to look at her as if they'd forgotten she was in the room.

"And before I make it, I have one question," she added.

"Go ahead," Walt said.

"If this guy has the envelope, why is he asking me for information?"

"Good question," Walt replied.

"Two people could be looking for the information," Gavin said. "One of them is looking and doesn't know the other one has already gotten his hands on it."

"You thinking partners who've turned on each other?" Walt asked, his eyes lighting up with interest.

"Could be, or the information is just so valuable that more than one person wants it."

Lexie couldn't believe what she was going to suggest, but she had to do it. "Then if this is ever to come to an end, it's even more important for me to go to the park. I admit I'm afraid, but I'll do it so Adam isn't living in fear all the time." She met Gavin's hard gaze. "With the protection your father has offered, that is."

"I'll put the plans into place." Walt charged out of the room.

Gavin watched him go for a moment then dropped back on the sofa and clutched her hands. "Don't do this, Lexie. Please."

She should pull her hands free, but she honestly liked his touch. "Do you disagree that making the drop is the best chance we've had so far to capture the killer?"

"No, it's a great opportunity, but I won't risk your life."

"Would you be on board with this plan if it involved someone other than me?"

"It would depend on the circumstances, but yes, I likely would." He tightened his grip. "But it *is* you, sugar, and I still care about you. I can't stand the thought of you getting hurt."

She reveled for a moment in his caring. In thinking that he might still love her. But it was precisely for that reason that she pulled free and went to look out the window to put distance between them. "If there's any chance that this will keep Adam safe, then I'm willing to take that chance."

"And what about a chance that you could die? How will that help Adam?"

She spun. "What are the odds that this person would shoot me before determining that I left him the correct information?"

"Not very good."

"Couple that with the vest and helmet, and I'm guessing it's extremely unlikely that I will die." She lifted her shoulders into a firm line. "I'm going, Gavin, and nothing you say will stop me."

THIRTEEN

Nerves near the breaking point, Lexie watched the bustle of activity from the sheriff's conference room. Walt had two deputies from Cypress County under his watchful eye as he instructed them on his expectations, while Matt hustled down the hallway carrying a vest and helmet. Gavin snatched the items from his brother's hands and gave them a thorough going-over.

Matt frowned, but walked away without commenting. Lexie was impressed that Matt was able to let Gavin take over like this without speaking out.

Gavin entered the room and placed the items on the table. "I don't like this. Not one bit. We haven't had enough time to strategize. What if there are loopholes in the plan? And I wasn't able to vet the deputies Dad's putting in place. How can I know if they're qualified?"

By the time he finished talking, his voice held rare panic that scared her. She'd never seen him like this. Never. Not even when she'd said no to a long-distance relationship. He'd changed in far more ways than his clothing. This extreme cautiousness and unease, when he had always been decisive and strong, broke her heart.

"Houston has changed you," she said.

He fisted his hands. "Why does everyone keep telling me that when it's not important?"

"Maybe because it's true. You're bordering on obsessive about taking care of every single detail."

"Well, you're wrong. It's not Houston. It's…" He clamped his mouth closed.

"It's what?"

He took a breath. Blew it out. Seemed to weigh his thoughts, then closed the door. "It's because of my big mistake here. With Dad. When I shot Emily. I can't let that happen again. Can't injure someone or let someone be injured on my watch. It'll…" He shook his head and his eyes filled with anguish so deep that Lexie's breath stilled.

She'd been wrong. Way wrong. If he was this distraught even three years after leaving his deputy job, he really had needed to quit working with his dad and step away. "I had no idea how deeply this affected you. And I only made things worse by getting angry at you for leaving town."

He watched her carefully. "I'm trying to get control of it. Trying to let down my guard and work with others, but when it comes to your safety…" He rubbed a hand over his face. "Man, it's worse than ever."

She laid a hand on his arm. "But here's the thing, Gavin. You've let your feelings sway you and moved to the other extreme. Might it keep you from acting when needed? Keep you from making a necessary decision for the right reasons?"

He grimaced. "You have a point."

"Then do an honest risk assessment here to decide if I should go."

He seemed to weigh it over. "You'll keep your head

down to prevent a direct shot to areas not protected by the ballistic helmet?"

"Yes."

"And you'll listen to me in your earbuds and react as I tell you? If I say abort, you'll abort."

"Yes," she promised.

"You won't linger."

"I'll do everything you've briefed me to do."

"Okay, then," he said, reluctance lingering in his tone. "I won't stand in your way."

She squeezed his arm, but he suddenly jerked her close and folded his strong arms around her. She rested her head against his broad chest and listened to his fast heartbeat. Felt the warmth of his arms. Remembered so many times when he'd held her in the past.

Then everything became clear—her hopes, her dreams, coming to the surface. She hadn't realized until now that she still hoped he would come home and they'd get back together. But now that she knew he needed to stay away from Lost Creek for his sanity, she had to let that dream go and forget about ever being with him.

She gently freed herself from his arms, the loss immediately carving out fresh pain in her heart. His gaze remained locked on her, even when Walt, carrying a communications system, opened the door. She took a step back.

Walt placed the items on the table. "Everything okay in here?"

She nodded.

"Then let's get you dressed."

"I'll do it." Gavin picked up the earbuds before his dad had a chance.

Walt nodded. "I'll double-check that we're ready on our end."

Lexie gaped at him.

"What's wrong?"

"For the first time since I've seen the two of you together again, you didn't argue with Gavin."

He glanced at Gavin and then back at her. "Seemed natural, I guess."

Gavin opened his mouth to speak then closed it and nodded instead. Walt offered a similar nod and left the room. They didn't say a word, but Lexie could tell the unspoken communication was a huge breakthrough.

Are You behind this, Father? she wondered, a flash of the faith she'd once clung to giving her hope.

Her heart sang for the progress. For both of them. For Winnie and Gavin's entire family. For herself, too?

Let it go. You know Gavin is never coming home.

"This is how you use the comms device." Gavin demonstrated, and she listened carefully to his directions.

Once the earbuds and cords were secured in place, he helped her with the vest, each touch of his fingers as he adjusted the Velcro giving her a fresh awareness of him.

She obviously still had feelings for him. Crazy, right? He might have had to leave town, but he'd still abandoned her. Exactly like her father's retreat after her mother died. That was a betrayal she'd never gotten over, and she likely wouldn't get over the same treatment from Gavin.

He settled the helmet on her head and reached for the straps, but she couldn't let him touch her any longer, so she stepped back to adjust them herself. He didn't seem to notice the change in her, just held out her jacket.

She quickly slipped her arms inside and moved away from him. She knew she was overreacting, but she couldn't let herself fall for him again. She couldn't take another abandonment. Just couldn't.

Gavin glanced at his watch. "We've got just enough

time to test out the audio and get the deputies in place. Then you'll drive over to the park in my car. We'll be a short distance away in the van, monitoring you. Got it?"

She nodded.

"Then let's go." He turned for the door then suddenly spun and grabbed her in another fierce hug. She could barely keep from lifting her face and asking him to kiss her, but she reminded herself that this hug was all about him gaining control of his concerns, not a demonstration of his love.

He let her go as quickly as he'd taken her into his arms and marched from the room. Outside, he climbed in the van to conduct audio tests. Then suddenly it was time for Lexie to step out on her own. She settled in his SUV and felt so alone. She'd claimed such confidence, but her hands shook as she cranked the engine and started down the road.

Keep it together. You're doing this for Adam.

She swallowed down the fear and drove to the park. Under overcast gray skies and a biting wind that kept most people indoors, she clutched the envelope tight and crossed the park. Her knees shook and sweat peppered her forehead. If the man was watching her, which she assumed he was, he had to see her protective gear. That also meant he'd know she'd reported the call to the sheriff. Could it have made him mad enough to shoot her? She wanted to look for him, but kept her head down as Gavin had instructed.

At the bin, she dropped the envelope inside. A sense of relief mixed with her fear, but she'd succeeded in her job, so she turned and hurried toward the exit.

On the sidewalk, the burner phone rang. She quickly answered, as she was sure the caller would praise her for following instructions.

"So you thought you could pull the wool over my eyes," the scrambled voice said.

What? "I don't know what you mean."

"I told you to come alone."

"I am alone."

"Please—do you think I'm stupid? That I wouldn't recognize Deputy Ulstad?"

"Deputy who?" she asked since she couldn't very well admit to not following his directions.

"You're ticking me off."

"Sorry." She did her best to sound like she meant it.

"Lucky for you, I'm giving you another chance. I'll contact you tomorrow and set up another drop. If you don't come alone, you'll pay with your life."

She stifled a gasp.

"And I suggest you retrieve the envelope before anyone finds it." He disconnected the call.

"Did you hear that?" she asked Gavin.

"Yes."

"Do I go back for the envelope?"

"I'll have Ulstad pick it up. You go straight to the car and back to Dad's office."

"On my way." She'd really angered the killer. Though he was giving her another chance, retaliation was a strong possibility, and the only thing she might have accomplished today was to put herself in even more danger.

As Gavin took the highway exit for the city of Cumberland to watch for Silas Ross, he glanced at Lexie in the passenger seat. She'd stared out the window in silence since they'd climbed into his SUV. A good thing or he might say something he shouldn't.

The minute he'd reached his dad's office to see her sitting with her arms wrapped around her waist and her beautiful blue eyes filled with fear, he'd had to fight from drawing her into his arms and never letting go. He'd already held her twice today. What message did that send? Was she thinking he wanted to get back together? Was he leading her on? Totally not fair to her and he needed to do a better job at keeping his distance.

"Do you really think Silas Ross could be our killer?" she asked.

"The caller recognized Ulstad, so that would suggest he lives in Cypress County, which—"

"Which is where Silas lives," she finished for him. "I wish we had more time to figure out the connection, but a second drop tomorrow doesn't leave much time."

"Dad and his team are working on it. If anyone can find the connection, they will," he said without thinking. Did he really feel that way or was it just a platitude to make her feel better?

She watched him as if she, too, saw the significance of his statement.

"If you're worried about tomorrow," he said, "the agents I called in to monitor the drop are very capable."

"Sounds like you have more confidence in them than you had in Deputy Ulstad."

"Not that Ulstad isn't capable, but I don't know him. I've worked with these agents for three years and know they're top-notch."

He parked in front of the clinic and sat back to wait for Ross to show up.

Gavin kept looking at his watch, the time ticking by slowly, but he wasn't about to start up a conversation and get distracted. About an hour after they arrived, Ross strolled down the street.

"There he is," he said.

Lexie sat forward, her hands clutched together in what looked like a death grip.

In his late twenties, the guy wore faded blue jeans and a black T-shirt under a leather bomber jacket. His hair was long, and when he entered the building, Gavin saw that it curled up in the back.

"Could he be the guy from the airstrip?" Gavin asked.

"He's the right size, and he has a similar confident strut."

"Then we'll wait for him to come out and have a chat with him so you can hear his voice."

If Gavin thought time had moved slowly before, it crept by at a snail's pace now. Just as he thought he'd crawl out of his skin, the door opened and Ross stepped out carrying a brown paper bag.

"Let's go." Gavin jumped out. He'd been worried that Ross would run when he saw him, but he didn't even notice them as he ripped open the bag to pull out a pill bottle. His hands shook as he tried to get it open.

"Silas Ross," Gavin said.

The guy's head popped up and surprise lit his face.

Either he was shocked that Gavin had caught on to him, or he was simply surprised to see Gavin back in the area.

Ross shoved the bottle into his pocket. "You back in town, McKade?"

He nodded and glanced at Lexie to see if she recognized the voice. She gave a shake of her head and Gavin's hope that Ross was their killer fizzled, but he could still provide a vital link to the Medicaid fraud.

Ross eyed him. "Doesn't look like you're a deputy."

"No. I work for the FBI." Gavin displayed his credentials. "That's why I'm here."

"To talk to me?" His voice squeaked high.

"I saw you come out of the doctor's office with those pills."

"So?"

"So I was wondering what they were for."

Ross eyed him. "That's none of your business."

Gavin held up his hands. "Hey, relax. You're not in any trouble. I'm interested in what the doctor is dispensing, that's all."

"Then you'll have to ask him." Ross backed away, watching Gavin as if waiting to be stopped.

Gavin had no probable cause to arrest Ross and had to let him go. He turned and bolted for his truck.

Gavin knew Ross would pop a pill as soon as possible and the lawman in him wanted to stop him from driving off. He might not be able to do anything, but others could. Gavin grabbed his phone to dial 9-1-1 to report a man potentially under the influence and provide Ross's license plate. He hung up and it took but a moment to realize that with Ross disappearing, so did another lead.

"Enough messing around. I'm going to go straight to the source." He jerked open the door and stepped back for Lexie to enter. He displayed his credentials and demanded to see Dr. Lowell immediately. The receptionist cringed, but got up and disappeared down a hallway.

Gavin wasn't going to let her warn Lowell and have him run out the back door.

"C'mon." He grabbed Lexie's hand and slipped through the door to a hallway.

Down the hall, he spotted Lowell talking to the receptionist. He wore thick glasses and a worried expression, which could mean something or could simply mean he was concerned that the FBI had come looking for him. Not unusual when people learned an agent wanted to talk to them.

Gavin didn't give the doctor a chance to go back into the room, but displayed his credentials and introduced them. "I need to ask you a few questions in private. Now."

Lowell nodded. "Follow me."

They went to a nicely appointed office and took seats around the desk.

Lowell leaned back in his chair. "What's this about?"

"Medicaid and drug fraud."

He blanched. "I don't know what you're talking about."

"That's not what Silas Ross just told us."

"Silas? I'm not sure—"

"C'mon, Doc. Don't give me the runaround. Silas just left your office, and he couldn't wait to take the narcotics you gave him then get in his truck and drive. Maybe injuring someone while under the influence. We have to stop him."

"He… I…" Lowell shoved his hand through his short gray hair. "I don't know what to say."

"How about telling me what's going on, and I'll make sure the DA knows you cooperated."

"Fine. I had financial issues, okay?" He shook his head. "My wife died suddenly. Heart attack. Let's just say I took it hard. Engaged in some pretty risky behavior to drown my sorrows. Racked up a big gambling debt that I couldn't pay and was going to lose the house. Maybe the practice. Then I remembered hearing about a doctor who'd bought a list of names to bill Medicaid. Got myself a list and my debt paid off."

He paused and snapped his chair forward. "I was going to stop billing then. I swear. But the hacker who sold me the list worked for a drug syndicate. They smuggled narcotics in from Mexico and distributed them through doctors. They threatened to expose the Medicaid thing if I didn't peddle their drugs."

"Wouldn't that just expose them?" Gavin asked.

His head shook with vehemence. "They had it set up so the two couldn't be connected."

If they were dealing with a drug syndicate out of Mexico, the danger to Lexie was even greater. Her worried expression said she understood that, too.

"How exactly does the program work?" he asked calmly to keep his rising concerns hidden.

"I'm given a list of patients who make an appointment. I set them up under one of the phony Medicaid names. I create a diagnosis that will keep them coming back on a regular basis and hand them the pills. They fork over the cash and I give it to the syndicate."

"How long has this been going on?" Gavin demanded.

"About two years, if you can believe that. Not that I didn't try to get out a few times, but they said they'd rather see me dead than let me walk around with knowledge of their operation."

Gavin didn't doubt that. "Who exactly are they?"

"I was never given names of syndicate members. I simply get calls via a burner phone, and I'm told where to pick up the drugs and leave the money. The location always varies. Each time I pick up the drugs, there's another phone waiting for me, and I destroy the current phone."

"How often do you meet?"

"Every few weeks, but it's not regular. It's their way of keeping me from planning anything. I'm due for one soon. Maybe this week, but I can never be sure."

Gavin couldn't sit back and wait for a potential drop to find the killer, but this was just the lead he needed in the fraud investigation. He pulled out his card. "I want you to call me the minute you receive the drop call. Got that?"

Lowell nodded. "Are you going to turn me in?"

"Not at this point if you listen and call me."

"You better believe I will."

Gavin stood. "I caution you not to mention this conversation to your contact. If they're as dangerous as you say, they'll kill you for meeting with me."

Lowell's color faded even more and Lexie's followed suit.

Gavin thought to warn Lowell, but his warning about the syndicate being extremely dangerous applied to Lexie, too, and there was no way to sugarcoat it for her.

FOURTEEN

Lexie washed the flour from her hands in the kitchen sink and stared out the window. She couldn't put the conversation with Dr. Lowell out of her mind. Had her father been involved with this drug syndicate, too? How could she reconcile that? Worse yet, how did she even move forward with such dangerous men after her? Did they think she was trying to bring them down? If so, when she couldn't produce this evidence, she and Adam would be in very grave danger. She'd asked Gavin about it in the car, but he'd simply said he had to process the news and then clammed up.

"Your mind has been somewhere else all afternoon," Betty said, interrupting Lexie's musings. "Is there anything I can help with?"

"Thank you—no." Lexie dried her hands. "Only Gavin can help."

"If it's about your relationship," Betty said matter-of-factly, "I hope the two of you have had a chance to talk it out. We'd all dearly love to see you as part of our family." She smiled, her wrinkly cheeks lifting and the skin tightening.

"Don't get your hopes up," Lexie cautioned. "Seems like Gavin isn't any closer to moving back here."

"But if he did, would you have him back?"

Lexie wasn't over his abandonment and couldn't pretend all was well with them, so she shook her head.

Betty frowned and placed her hands on Lexie's shoulders. "Life's too short to waste time. If you still love my grandson, I urge you to work things out with him." She took a long look into Lexie's eyes then drew her close for a hug. She smelled of cinnamon from the snickerdoodles they'd been baking, and the familiar scent of Gavin's favorite cookies brought tears to Lexie's eyes.

She loved this woman. All of the McKades. But was that enough to let go of the deep ache she still felt over Gavin deserting her? After all, with her father gone, no one was stopping her from moving to Houston if Adam was agreeable to such a move. But could she trust Gavin not to leave her over something else?

Betty stepped back. "I've said my piece, and I won't interfere again. I'm leaving it in God's hands and I know He has big things planned for you both."

"Thank you for caring," Lexie said, wishing she thought the same thing, as she didn't think God had plans for her at all.

Betty squeezed Lexie's hand. "You go find Gavin, and I'll finish up the cookies."

"Are you sure?"

She nodded. "Might want to bring a plate of cookies to him, though."

Lexie filled a plate and went to the office where he was reviewing files to see if he could find any connection between Dr. Lowell and her father.

He looked up from behind his computer and smiled, looking heart-stoppingly handsome. "Please tell me those are snickerdoodles."

Speechless over the return of the good-natured Gavin, she nodded and set the plate next to him.

He snatched up a cookie, his smile disappearing as he chomped a bite and moaned with joy.

She loved seeing him as carefree as he'd been before the shooting. Oh, how she wished he could let go of his past to find this kind of contentment again. Not for her. But for him. To find the peace he needed to be whole again.

He swallowed. "I know these aren't traditional Christmas cookies, but you've gotta love Nana for adding them to her Christmas baking list because she knows I love them."

"She spoils all of you so much." Lexie sat before she did something dumb like lean over the desk and kiss him.

"She says that's what nanas are for." His silly boyish grin that Lexie had seen in many of his family portraits crossed his face.

Lexie understood his emotions. She'd once been spoiled by Betty, too. Even after she and Gavin had broken up, Betty had dropped by with freshly baked goodies until Lexie told her it was too hard to see her. She wished she'd known her grandparents, but they'd all passed and she could hardly remember them.

"So are you trying to butter me up for something with these cookies?" He took another one.

"No. I was on my way to talk to you about Dr. Lowell, and Betty told me to bring them to you."

His smile disappeared. "What about Lowell?"

"If my dad was involved in the Medicaid fraud, might he have escalated to dealing illegal drugs, too?"

"Seems quite possible."

"What if he'd tried to get out from under their control like Dr. Lowell, and they threatened to kill him? Perhaps the very reason he turned the three patients away when he did."

"Sounds plausible and could also be the reason he disappeared," Gavin said. "But there's a difference in that Lowell didn't have a family where your dad did."

"Family? I don't see how that would make a difference."

"Your dad was worth more alive and peddling their drugs than dead, so it's likely they'd threaten to kill you and Adam first."

"But when Dad took off, wouldn't they have approached us?"

"I could be wrong, or maybe when he disappeared they didn't see any point in threatening you until your dad came back to town."

"So maybe Dad didn't try to get out. Or he might not have been involved in the same syndicate and this is about something else entirely." She thought for a moment. "One thing is certain... Dad's killer said he was involved in a syndicate, and he was going to meet with the leader. But what about?"

"I suppose he could have found a way to collect information on them, and they left him alone because he could turn them in."

"And Dad put the information in the envelope. He'd said it was my insurance, so that makes sense."

"This all sounds plausible, but they were so careful to avoid giving Lowell any information. Your dad would have had to be crafty to gather anything on them."

"Well, Dad was a crafty guy. He could have followed the guy with the phone, or even paid someone to follow him. I could totally see him doing that if these men were putting pressure on him. He had such a big ego, he didn't back down from anyone, maybe not even these guys."

"You could be right, but at this point we have no proof."

Lexie's phone rang but she didn't recognize the number. Thinking it could have to do with her father's funeral arrangements, she answered.

"Ms. Grant, this is Dr. Thomas. Medical examiner."

"Yes, Dr. Thomas, how can I help you?" she asked, but wasn't sure she wanted to hear what he had to report.

"I've completed your father's autopsy and thought you might be interested in my findings. You likely already know this, but I discovered a mass in his brain. Cancerous and inoperable. If he hadn't been shot, he would've had a month or so left."

"Cancer. Dad?" She let the news settle in. "Is it possible that he wouldn't have known about it?"

"Not likely. At the cancer's advanced stage, he couldn't have explained away the symptoms. Especially with his medical knowledge."

Lexie's heart clenched and she couldn't think of a single word in response. Even when her father knew he was dying, he hadn't wanted to spend his last days with her. With Adam. Her heart creased and tears pricked her eyes.

"Also," the ME continued, "the body's been released, and you can now arrange for the funeral home to transport him."

"Thank you, Dr. Thomas." She ended the call.

"What is it?" Gavin asked.

She managed to tell him about the call before her tears took her to a place she didn't want to go.

Gavin came around the desk and knelt at her feet. He took her hands.

"How could he not want to be with me in his final days? Am I that horrible? Unlovable?" She didn't care if Gavin saw her distress, but let her tears fall, her body heaving with the pain. She freed her hands and wrapped her arms around her body to rock in place.

"Look at me, sugar," Gavin demanded.

His sharp tone snapped her from her reverie and she peered at him.

He gently pried her arms free and held her hands, the warmth of his touch comforting. "You're an amazing woman, Lex. He was a fool if he didn't love you enough to spend his last days with you."

She thought to mention that Gavin had done the same thing in leaving her, but she couldn't battle that pain now, too, so she kept her mouth shut.

"You know," he said, "maybe he left because he loved you."

"How's that even possible?"

"What if he feared the syndicate was coming after him, and he left so they'd hunt him down and leave you and Adam alone?"

Was that possible? "But wouldn't they still come after us to see if we knew where he was?"

"I suppose they might have. Maybe he explained all of this in his will, and you should consider reading it."

"I'll think about it," she said and freed her hands to wipe away her tears.

Could she honestly handle it if her father didn't mention her at all? If he hadn't said goodbye and had left because he just didn't love her?

Gavin tried to sleep on the lumpy sofa in the cabin, but he couldn't let go of his conversation with Lexie that afternoon. His heart ached for Lexie. How could she not realize what an amazing woman she was?

He wished she'd agree to get her father's will. Even if she was right and her father hadn't wanted to be with her in his dying days, it was better to know about it so she could move on.

At least, that was what he'd want to do if it was his dad. Man, thinking about his dad dying was a kick in the teeth. Would he really want to know his father resented him until his last breath? That they hadn't reconciled. How could Gavin live with that? But this wasn't about him and how he would feel if he lost his father.

It wasn't even about reconciling so he could come back home and be with Lexie. It was about now. Today. About how he and his dad couldn't talk to one another. Couldn't comfortably be in the same room together. And it was also about his mom, the whole family, in the middle of their feud, suffering.

They'd made a bit of progress today, if his dad's earlier nod when readying Lexie for the meet meant what Gavin had thought it meant. So was it the right time to approach him to try to work this out?

Gavin just didn't know. He sighed and turned over. Forced his mind to still and listen to the whistling wind. He fell into an uneasy sleep until a noise woke him.

Shivering, he lurched forward and discovered the room was freezing cold. Had the noise been in his dreams or had something happened to the heater? He got to his feet and slipped into his boots before grabbing his holster and clipping it on his belt. He took a few steps when the strong smell of propane gas stopped him dead in his tracks.

Propane powered the stove and heater, which seemed to be out. He raced across the room to the stove, the smell growing stronger as he approached the kitchen.

The knobs were all turned off, but the smell came from behind the stove.

No! Oh, no. He's trying to poison her.

Gavin bolted for the bedrooms and pounded on the doors. "Get up! Gas! The place could explode!"

He heard movement behind Lexie's door but not Adam's. Gavin shoved the door open and jerked earbuds out of the kid's ears. "Get up. There's a propane leak. We have to leave."

He stumbled out of bed.

"Meet me at the door." Gavin ran back to the living area, where Lexie hurried to the front door and was slipping into her boots. Adam joined them. With one swipe of his hand, Gavin pulled all of their jackets from the hooks and tossed theirs to them.

"Stay here for a moment while I take a look outside." He stepped out to check for a trap. He peered around the vicinity while shrugging into his jacket.

Thinking it was safer outside than in, he turned back to them. "C'mon. Let's move."

The moment Lexie stepped outside he grabbed her hand. "We're going to run all the way to the main house." He looked at Adam. "Can you keep up?"

"Yes."

Gavin started running, but kept checking to make sure the boy was in step with them. His free hand on his sidearm, he led them to the house and unlocked the door.

"What happened, anyway?" Adam asked, his eyes filled with fear.

"A noise woke me, and I smelled propane. It was coming from the stove area."

"But we didn't use the stove."

"Exactly," Gavin said. "Wake Dad up and tell him what's going on and to call 9-1-1."

"Why can't you do that?" she asked.

"I'm going back to the propane tank to turn it off and warn the other guests."

"Isn't it dangerous to go back there?" she asked.

"The tank is a distance from that cabin, so I'll be fine."

Lexie looked like she might cry, but instead she drew him close for a hug. "Be careful."

"Always."

He headed for the stairs and heard Adam ask, "So you're hugging him now? Unbelievable."

Gavin's gut twisted as he ran across the property. He soon reached the large propane tank and turned the lever. He wanted to go into the cabin to confirm the propane source, but he wasn't foolish.

He woke the other guests and evacuated them a safe distance away. By the time sirens sounded from the fire trucks, his dad came barreling down the drive.

"You're okay." He sighed out a breath.

"Fine," he said, his mind now turning to what could have happened if he hadn't woken up. He could have lost Lexie. Adam. His own life. Lexie was right. He didn't have all the time in the world to fix things. Not only with his dad, but with everyone.

God, please. If You're there. Listening. I can't keep hurting my family. Lexie and Adam or myself. This has gone on long enough. Bring it to an end. Please. I'm ready. More than ready.

Gavin heard the fire truck stop nearby and hurried over to update Lieutenant Frazer. Carrying a device to read propane levels, the lieutenant entered the cabin while his men stood at the ready.

Frazer soon stepped outside and, after talking to one of his men, joined Gavin. "The propane levels are high, but the place isn't gonna blow. We'll add fans to suck out the fumes and I'll monitor things. Not that a carbon monoxide detector can pick up propane, but you might want to consider installing a propane alarm."

"We did install them," Gavin's dad said. "In each unit, near the stove."

"Then someone removed it." Frazer frowned. "But your location was spot-on, as the leak came from the stove."

"But I checked it," Gavin insisted. "Everything was turned off."

"True," Frazer replied. "Someone disconnected the main line."

"So this was no accident." Gavin let the deadly implication settle in. "No accident at all."

FIFTEEN

Gavin spent the morning getting agents up to speed and in place for the envelope drop while Lexie met with Aunt Ruth, who'd returned from vacation. Now he sat in the van with his father and watched Lexie on the large monitor. She marched up to the new drop location at the post office, and he could hardly sit still. The past few days told him he wasn't over her and that she still meant the world to him. How could he possibly rest easy with her in danger?

"I have to admit this case has me baffled," his dad said. "If our suspect was expecting Lexie to provide the information today, he wouldn't have tried to kill her last night."

"Unless he found the info between the time he called her and bedtime last night, and he no longer needs her."

"But why kill her?"

Gavin wondered the same thing. "He could think she'd read the files and he had to silence her before she told anyone. Like maybe the second guy we suspect is involved. Or maybe he thinks she's double-crossing him to try to catch him, and the attempt on her life is all about revenge."

"That would make sense, but where could he have

found the files?" His father frowned. "If we don't apprehend the guy on this drop, I'll head back to Ruth's house to see if anyone's been there since Betty and Winnie cleaned up."

"Sounds like a plan." Gavin shifted his attention to the screen where Lexie tossed the envelope in the trash can and walked away. She soon stepped out of camera range. Gavin wished she could talk to him as she walked to the car and assure him of her safety, but that would alert the guy if he was watching.

Each moment he waited felt like an hour. He counted. Waited. Prayed. Yeah, him. Praying again. Maybe believing a little, too.

"I'm at the car," she finally said. "Any action?"

Gavin sighed heavily, his relief riding on the gust of air. "Not yet. Head back to the office and let me know the second you arrive."

His stress level dropped a notch. He didn't fully relax until the next call from Lexie came in. But just then a man dressed in a parka with the hood up, his head down, moved furtively down the street, grabbing Gavin's attention. The oversize parka seemed too severe even for the cold snap. It was as if he was wearing it to disappear within the huge hood. He paused near the trash can and took out his cell phone. Acting as if he was simply talking on the phone, he leaned over and grabbed the envelope.

"Move in," Gavin instructed his agents.

"You have him?" Lexie asked.

"Looks like it."

The agents slipped out of the shadows and grabbed the man. He resisted arrest, but the agents soon had him on the ground and in cuffs. They jerked him to his feet and pulled off his hood. He had slicked-back hair and a spotty beard, and was generally well-groomed.

Roiling emotions ground through Gavin's gut and he had to restrain himself from leaping out of the truck to tear into the man.

Matt arrived to take the suspect into custody. He pulled a phone from the guy's pocket and then tapped the screen a few times. "It's the phone used to call Lexie," Matt reported over the comms unit. "I'm bringing this jerk in."

"We have him!" Lexie cried out.

"Don't get too excited, Lex," Gavin warned as his father got their van on the road.

They arrived at the office and Lexie met them in the hallway. A male, cursing at the top of his lungs from the back entrance, declared his innocence in the arrest. Lexie's eyes widened and then she clapped a hand over her mouth.

"What's wrong?" Gavin asked, peering worriedly down at her.

"If that's the man you arrested, he's not the man from the airport. Not the man who killed Dad."

"Are you sure?"

She nodded, her eyes going wide. "So this isn't over."

"Let's not jump to conclusions," his father said. "The interview could clear things up."

Gavin nodded. "We'll talk to him right away."

"Will you come back to update me when you finish?" She clutched Gavin's arm.

"Of course." He squeezed her hand then followed his father to the interview room.

"Meet Yancy Vandale," Matt said as he settled the suspect in a chair. "He's the pharmacist at Speedy Pharmacy in Willow."

Eager to figure out how a pharmacist was involved,

Gavin gestured for his dad to sit in the chair across the table from Vandale.

He shook his head. "It's all yours, son."

Gavin couldn't hide his surprise, but quickly recovered and took the chair to begin questioning.

Matt departed, and his dad leaned against the wall. If Gavin read him right, he appeared confident in Gavin's ability. Maybe his dad *had* changed, after all.

Gavin turned his attention to the suspect. "You're in a lot of trouble, Mr. Vandale."

He scoffed. "For picking up an envelope out of a trash can. Not hardly."

"Your comment might fly if you weren't carrying the burner phone used to call Ms. Grant and threaten her."

Vandale tried to cross his arms but the cuffs prevented it, so he jutted out his chin in defiance.

Gavin sat higher. "Take that attitude, and you'll soon be going away for murdering Dr. Grant."

His mouth fell open. "I didn't kill the guy. He was alive and kicking when I left him at the airstrip."

His statement almost knocked Gavin off his chair. "So you admit to meeting him at the airstrip?"

"Yeah, I…well…guess I shouldn't have said that. But I didn't kill him."

"So you didn't take the envelope, then?"

He paused for a moment as if searching for the right answer. "The only envelope I took is the one I picked up today."

"What was your connection to the doctor?"

Vandale sat quietly for a moment then shrugged. "I'm done talking until you cut me a deal."

"The only thing on the table is us telling the DA that you cooperated," Gavin said, but his father would have to arrange it, as Gavin wouldn't give a guy who'd stalked Lexie a break. "And that offer expires in thirty seconds."

"Fine. That'll have to do." Vandale took a breath and let it out slowly. "Dr. Grant wrote Medicaid prescriptions for me. I didn't dispense the meds but billed Medicaid. Was pure profit."

More Medicaid fraud. Unbelievable. "Why would Dr. Grant do that?"

"For a kickback. Said he was going to live like a king in retirement. Then he disappeared and I kinda freaked out. Thought maybe you all were onto him, and he left information about our little side business behind. So I looked for the files."

"Starting with ransacking Dr. Grant's office and home right after he disappeared," Gavin clarified. "And more recently Ms. Grant's truck and Ruth Paulson's house."

"Yeah. I mean, I had to know."

"But you didn't find anything," Gavin prompted.

He shook his head. "And with Grant missing it worried me sick. Then out of the blue the doc calls me. Tells me he's coming back to town to meet with his daughter. Says he wants the money I owe him in cash or he'll hand over proof of my fraud to the authorities."

Odd. "Why would he do that when it would implicate him, too?"

"He was bluffing. He told me at the airstrip that he was dying and claimed he'd destroyed all the Medicaid information so no one would find it. He just wanted me to show up and give him the money from the last quarter."

"But you were still worried that he didn't destroy the records and Ms. Grant had them."

"Thought she might find something when she went through his stuff. Had to push her to see." Vandale slunk down in his chair.

"Tell me why I should believe you didn't kill the doc."

"I'm not a killer—that's why."

"Or are you just trying to avoid charges even more serious than defrauding our government?"

Vandale sat forward as if suddenly realizing he was in serious trouble. "Look. You have to believe me. For one, I don't even own a gun. And two, I wouldn't have any idea how to blow up a plane. I was as shocked when that happened as you. I mean, the fireball was huge."

"You were still at the airport when it exploded?" Gavin asked.

"Didn't trust Grant. So I hung around to see what he was up to."

"You witnessed the murder, then."

He nodded. "Some dude on a dirt bike. Skinny. Crazy. Hiding behind his face shield." Vandale shook his head. "Could hardly believe what I was seeing. Then you rode up, so I took off. I was going to leave a phone and message for Lexie at her house, but I saw her truck. Figured right after seeing her daddy die, leaving the phone in her truck would scare her even more, so when I contacted her, she'd comply."

Gavin fisted his hands and had to breathe deep to keep his anger in check. "But you saw the killer take the envelope. It could have held your information."

"Could have, but the killer was focused on a syndicate. That had nothing to do with me."

Gavin had heard all he'd needed to hear. This wasn't their killer. Especially since his voice didn't match the man Lexie had heard. He got to his feet.

"Book him," he said. He left his dad to move Vandale into lockup and went to the conference room to update Lexie.

Her eyes lit up when he entered the room. "What did he say?"

Gavin explained his connection to her father.

She took in all the information, her expression tightening with his every word. "Seriously, Dad was involved in prescription fraud, too?"

"Again, we have no proof, but I have no reason to think Vandale is lying."

Her phone rang, snagging her attention. "It's Ruth. I asked her to pick Adam up from school so I could be here, and to call me when they got to Trails End."

Lexie answered, her love for Ruth burning in her eyes. Gavin couldn't help but be reminded of the days when she'd looked at him with such love, too.

She listened for only a moment and her face went deadly pale. "No, no. That's not possible. Are you sure?" She grabbed on to the wall.

"What's wrong?" Gavin asked, his cell ringing in the tone he'd assigned to Deputy Erickson.

"It's Adam." The words came out in a strangled cry. "He's missing."

The room spun. Lexie couldn't breathe. Her brother was missing. Gone. No one knew where. She was hyperventilating and her legs wouldn't hold her, so she slid down the wall and landed on the floor with a bone-jarring thump.

Gavin rushed to her side, took her hand, and she let him hold fast. Walt entered the room and Gavin filled him in on the development.

"How in the world did Erickson lose the kid?" Walt shouted.

"That's what I'd like to know."

"I'll call Erickson." Walt snapped his phone from the belt holder.

Lexie watched him like she was in an out-of-body experience. She felt numb. Lost. Like she couldn't do a thing. But she had to do something to protect her baby brother, right? But what?

"C'mon, sugar. Let's get you to a chair." Gavin helped her across the room, his warm arm around her back thawing a bit of her frozen state.

"Let me get you some water," he said and stepped into the hallway.

As if water could help her. Help Adam. She was a basket case. But she was no good to Adam this way. Ruth had few details to share except that she'd arrived to discover he was gone, and Deputy Erickson hadn't known he was missing. They'd called Adam's cell, but he hadn't answered.

That's it. Maybe he knew he was in trouble and wouldn't answer for them, but might take her call. She grabbed her phone and dialed him.

"C'mon, bud, pick up," she whispered, her heart shattering into tiny pieces as it continued to ring then went to voice mail. She left a frantic message, then stared at the phone in her hand while trying to come up with where he could be.

Gavin returned with the water and gently pried the phone from her hand. "We'll find him."

Would they? She took a sip of the water, but could barely swallow.

Walt hung up and came to sit across from her. "Erickson said he went out for a smoke. Two minutes was all, but he had to step off the property so he didn't violate school rules. He kept the front door in sight, but when he came back, Adam was gone. All-fire stupid thing to do." Walt slammed a fist on the table, sloshing the water.

Gavin jerked in response. For all Lexie knew, it reminded him of the way his dad had reacted when Emily was shot.

Gavin stood. "I'll head straight over to the school to look at surveillance videos."

"Don't bother," Walt said. "Budget cuts kept them from installing them."

"Then I'll interview teachers and students."

"I'm going with you." Lexie struggled to her feet.

Gavin opened his mouth, but she wasn't about to let him waste time trying to talk her out of it. "I'm going. Period. No discussion."

"I wasn't going to argue," he said gently. "Let's go."

Walt got up. "I'll be right behind you, and I'll get Matt and Tessa over there, too."

Her legs still felt wobbly, so she let Gavin help her to the SUV. He quickly got them on the road toward the school with sirens and lights running, but despite the noise and flashing lights, it still seemed to take forever to get across town to the school. What if they were too late and something awful had happened to him?

Lexie took several deep breaths, trying to calm her nerves. She had to focus on finding Adam…not jump to the worst-case scenario. "With Vandale in custody, this proved there really are two suspects."

"Vandale could have hired someone to take Adam," he countered.

"But why would he do that if he thought he was getting the information from me today?"

"After we gather facts, I'll question Vandale again." Gavin blew out a breath. "Who knows? We could arrive to find out Adam was just in the bathroom. Or cut class and he's fine."

She shot him a questioning look. "Do you really believe that?"

"I don't know what to believe." He slammed a fist on the steering wheel. "I can't fathom the thought of anything bad happening to the kid. I love him, you know. And this happened on *my* watch."

What? Love? She'd known he'd once loved her little brother, but hearing him say he still did gave her hope she had no business embracing. Even if her heart wanted to go there, she had to let it go until after Adam was found and she could think about it. "This didn't happen on your watch but on Erickson's."

"Don't give me an out, Lexie. I'm in charge of your and Adam's protection."

"Actually, that would be your dad."

"No! Stop! Don't give me an excuse. This is my fault. You can't convince me otherwise." He swung into the parking lot.

Lexie didn't wait for the SUV to stop rocking before bolting outside and starting up the walkway.

"Hold up," Gavin called out, his footfalls pounding closer. "This could be a trap to get you here, and I want you by my side."

He slid an arm around her waist to draw her close. They moved quickly, bursting through the door to find Deputy Erickson waiting for them.

"Any updates?" Gavin asked.

"I located one of Adam's friends. She said he got a text from Lexie telling him she'd pick him up early and to meet her in the back parking lot."

Lexie stared at the man responsible for her brother's absence. "I didn't text him, and he's a smart kid. He'd know the text didn't come from my phone."

"Supposedly the text said you had to get another phone because yours was tapped. Adam bought the story and was glad to get out of school even a few minutes early, so he readily followed the directions."

"What time did these texts arrive?" Gavin asked.

"The friend said two thirty or so." Erickson worried his lip between his teeth.

Lexie changed her focus to Gavin. "Then Vandale couldn't have sent them."

"Doesn't mean he didn't have someone else do it for him," Gavin replied. "In fact, maybe he planned this in case anything went wrong at the drop. Then he would have leverage to try to get us to release him."

"I'm sorry, Lexie," Erickson said. "This is all my fault. I shouldn't have left the school."

Lexie agreed, but she also knew people were fallible. Like when Emily had been shot. Gavin hadn't meant her any harm. He'd only wanted to help. So had Erickson. "Just help us find him."

Ruth came out from the office, her face pale, her hands shaking. "I don't know what to do. Tell me what to do."

Lexie had never seen her strong aunt shaken like this, and it upped Lexie's own anxiety. What were they going to do? She didn't know, but calling out for God's help felt like the right thing to do.

SIXTEEN

Striking out on any other leads at the school, Gavin drove Lexie back to Trails End. They hung their jackets in the silent house, and he felt his family's absence acutely. While Tessa combed the school for forensic leads, everyone else had hurried into town to help man the phones at his dad's office. They were calling students just in case someone had seen something and could provide additional information on Adam's whereabouts.

Lexie wanted to make calls, too, but Gavin and his father agreed that they needed to slow down, review the investigation and work on a more expansive plan to find Adam. Since Lexie knew him best, they wanted her in on the discussion, too. But lingering in the office and continuing to hear call after call that didn't produce a lead had raised her panic level, so they'd returned to the ranch to talk.

Gavin wished Ruth could be there with Lexie, but they'd sent her home with a deputy to monitor the landline. If Adam had been abducted, and all signs were pointing that way, and the kidnapper wanted to contact Lexie but didn't have her cell number, he would call the house.

His father's phone rang and broke the silence. He answered and dread filled Gavin's gut.

"Hold on, Larry," his dad said. "Nothing about Adam, but I have to take this call." He went down the hall toward his office.

"Let's go in the dining room." Gavin gently took her arm and escorted her into the room.

They settled in chairs and Gavin kept his focus on Lexie. With each passing moment, her distress escalated and he hoped the conversation didn't make things more difficult for her.

She folded her hands on the table. "Do you think Vandale's lying and he hired someone to help him?"

"No way to be sure at this point," Gavin said. "But since kidnapping carries such stiff penalties, it seems pretty aggressive just to cover up a simple white-collar crime. My gut says Vandale's issues are unrelated to the envelope, and we need to keep our focus on the patient billing fraud."

She nodded.

"Still," Gavin said, "it's important to keep the burner phone with you in case the kidnapper is connected to Vandale and he uses that phone."

Lexie dug both phones from her pockets and placed them on the table. "Why doesn't he call already?"

"He could be drawing this out to make you suffer so when he does call, you'll jump to do his bidding and give him the information."

"I can't, though." She grabbed Gavin's arm. "I don't have what he wants, and he'll kill Adam. I can't lose him, too."

"Don't cry, sugar." He rested his hands over hers when all he wanted to do was to lift her into his arms and promise he'd fix this for her. "We'll find Adam."

"How can you be so sure?"

He couldn't, but then, he wouldn't tell her that, either, so he continued to hold her hand and prayed for Adam's safety.

Lexie sat staring out the window for how long, Gavin didn't know. He couldn't sit and do nothing, so he got up. Paced. And thought things through. Grasping for anything they might know to locate Adam. But what? What rock had they left unturned?

The will.

He pivoted to face Lexie. "Your dad's will could contain information to point us in the right direction."

"Wouldn't Mike Alexander bring it to our attention if it did?"

"Confidentiality might keep him from revealing anything. Or if your dad left a sealed envelope for you, Mike wouldn't know what it held."

"You think?" Her face brightened for a moment, and then the hope vanished. "But I can't… I mean hearing… I—"

"What if I read it so you don't have to?" he offered, as he knew where her thoughts were going.

"Yes, that would be perfect."

"Then give Mike a call while I see if Dad will go pick it up."

"Can you go?" she asked. "I feel silly enough about not taking care of this myself, and I don't want to send the sheriff to run an errand for me."

"He cares about you, Lex, and he wouldn't mind."

"Still, I'd feel better if you'd do it."

She wanted something from him. Exactly what he'd been hoping. Maybe not this particular thing, but there was no way he'd say no. He'd be gone for thirty minutes at most, and if a half hour might help repair the rift between them, then it was worth the risk of being gone when the kidnapper called. Besides, if the kidnapper phoned, his dad could immediately notify him.

"You get hold of Mike, and I'll ask Dad if he can stay home long enough for me to pick up the will."

She picked up her phone and Gavin started for the office. It felt weird to be going to ask his father for a favor. Even odder, that he trusted his father to keep Lexie safe. But surprisingly he did. Completely.

His dad was stowing his phone on his belt clip when Gavin stepped through the doorway.

"Something new happen?" he asked.

"No, but I'm wondering if Dr. Grant might have left a letter to Lexie with his will that might explain things."

"Good thinking. You call Mike to bring it out here."

Gavin had let his emotions to help Lexie color his thinking and miss this obvious solution. Still, he wasn't going to back out on telling her he'd go. "Lexie wants me to head into town to pick it up."

"It's not a good idea to take Lexie into town."

"I totally agree, which is why I wanted to ask if you can stay here to keep an eye on her."

"Me? You want me to handle her protection?"

Gavin nodded and their gazes locked. He'd have to be blind to miss the burgeoning look of hope and pride in his father's eyes. Another good reason for Gavin to go to town. He could start repairing the rift with his dad, too.

Emotions raced through Gavin and he cleared his throat to ward them off. "Unless, of course, you have something else you need to do."

"Of course not. I'll do whatever I can for that little girl. You know that, right?"

Gavin nodded.

"It's none of my business, but you ever think maybe it was a mistake to let her go?"

"I didn't let her go. I wanted to try for a long-distance relationship until Adam went off to college, but she didn't want to have anything to do with me." Gavin couldn't believe he was sharing the details of his breakup with his father, of all people.

"I can see that." He quickly held up a hand. "Not that I'm judging you for your decision, but after the way her daddy hurt her, your leaving had to do a number on her."

"Yeah," he said, but didn't know what else to say.

Fortunately, Lexie poked her head into the room.

His dad smiled at her. "Sounds like you and I are going to hold down the fort for a little while."

"Thank you," she said.

"Hey, no problem." His dad was doing his best to sound cheerful, but a hard edge rode under the tone, giving Gavin reassurance that his father was taking this duty seriously.

"I just need a piece of paper to write out a letter authorizing Gavin to pick up the will," Lexie said.

"Still keep paper in the top drawer?" Gavin asked as memories of coming in to get paper to draw as a kid assaulted him.

"Yep."

Gavin pulled open the drawer and it hit him then how very much he wanted God's help to reconcile with his dad and regain his relationship with his family. It would have to wait until they brought Adam safely home and the killer was behind bars, which he prayed they would do, but wanting the change was half the battle, right?

Lexie couldn't sit there staring at the phones. Walt was in the office taking care of whatever business Larry had called about. The sheriff loved coffee, so she went to the kitchen to brew a pot in thanks for his support. She set the phones on the table and got the coffee brewing. While she waited, she decided to load the dishwasher with baking dishes that Betty had left behind in her rush to leave.

Lexie soon completed her task when her phone chimed. She turned to discover her phone lit up and rushed to the table. She found a new text with a video but no message from a number she didn't recognize. She opened the file. It started loading, a circle spinning on the screen as fast as the thoughts in her head. The video cleared, and at the sight of the image filling the screen, she gasped. Weakness invaded her body and she dropped the phone.

"No, oh, no." She scrambled to pick it up. "Please let it work."

She tapped it and the screen came to life. "Thank you!"

She watched the short video of her brother gagged and handcuffed to a bar on a worn, slatted wall.

Her brother. A captive. Prisoner. She thought she might be sick and dropped to the chair. Panted to catch her breath. To think.

There was no message, sound or request—why? Maybe to torment her more. Was that even possible?

She sat staring. Playing the video over and over, trying to make out the location. Willing the phone to chime again. When it did, she jumped.

Don't tell anyone about this text. Come alone to meet me, and I'll let Adam go. If you're not here in thirty minutes, he dies.

A chill pierced her heart. He was going to kill Adam. Kill him if she didn't join him. Her brother. Her poor little brother. Bound. Gagged. Needing her. Needing her now!

She'd bolt out the door right now if she thought Walt

would let her go, but if he heard her, he'd come after her. Just the opposite of the kidnapper's demand, likely ensuring that he would kill Adam.

She thumbed in a response to buy time to think.

Can't get away. The sheriff's being extra vigilant.

Are you sure? I made sure the sheriff and his men are far too busy to notice you.

What in the world did this guy mean? Did he know something she didn't?

She had to check on Walt. She silently crept down the hall.

He paced his office, his phone to his ear. "What do you mean Vickson's old house exploded? Why would someone blow up an abandoned house? Are we looking at a bomb here?"

A bomb. A perfect distraction—and it fit with the profile of the guy who blew up the plane. A guy who now had her brother. Her heart constricted and she glanced at Walt one more time.

He was indeed distracted, and she had to believe the kidnapper had set the explosion for that very reason.

She was free to go to Adam. To save him. She grabbed her jacket from the foyer peg and rushed back to the kitchen to text the kidnapper, asking where she was to meet him.

He provided a rural address not too far away.

On my way, she replied, her fingers trembling so hard she had to use autocorrect to send the simple message.

Calm down, she warned herself. *Adam needs you calm. Not a basket case.*

She pulled in a deep breath. Let it out. Took another

and then grabbed the keys for the ranch truck from the holder by the back door. She quietly slipped out of the house and ran for the truck. Near the stable, she paused to lift her face.

God, please. Please let me be doing the right thing and make sure the kidnapper releases Adam as he promised.

She climbed into the truck, and thankfully, it fired on the first try, so maybe Walt hadn't heard it start.

When she made it to the narrow, rutted road leading to her destination and no sirens sounded behind her, she heaved a sigh of relief that she'd gotten away without being detected. She drove for several miles then pulled off the road onto a weed-infested lot. She got out and childhood memories came racing back.

The property owned by an oil company held abandoned drilling equipment. Most notably, an old, wooden oil storage tank that Lexie estimated at twenty feet high. One of her classmates had gotten stuck in it when she was in second grade. The oil company had put a lid on the open tank the next day and removed the ladder. They claimed it was cheaper than cleaning up the oil residue. They'd also fenced the property with barbed wire, but as Lexie approached, she discovered the wire had been cut.

She spotted a Honda Accord parked farther in. It had to be the car Gavin had seen at the overlook. She made her way down a path of knee-high grass flattened from foot traffic. The sound of a generator or pump drew her attention to a small storage shed. The door opened and a man stepped out.

"Where's Adam?" she screamed at him.

He faced her, a gun in his hand. She instantly recognized him from when she'd passed the fire pit at the cabin. He was staying at the dude ranch. He'd been there right under their noses all along. Right next door.

Anger started flowing through her body. "Where's my brother?"

"All in due time."

She gasped. It was him. The man from the airfield. The killer. Standing right in front of her. A murderer, and he had Adam.

"My brother?" she demanded, though fear invaded her every cell.

"Like I said, you'll see him soon."

She had to believe him, as thinking that he could have killed Adam wasn't something she could bear. "Who are you?"

"Name's Dean Wilcox."

Fear fought to take control, but she swallowed hard. "Is your name supposed to mean something to me?"

"Not likely, but it should. I'm your brother."

"Brother? You're nuts. I only have one brother."

"That you know about." He scoffed. "Dear old Dad got my mom pregnant before he married your mother. Left my mother in a lurch. Alone and penniless."

"I don't believe you."

"Figured you'd be just like Dad." He pulled a folded piece of paper from his jacket pocket. "Had to show him the DNA results, too. Not that it mattered. He still didn't care and wouldn't acknowledge me."

Dean handed over the paper and she took a long look at it. He could have faked the document, but he was angry enough for her to believe him. She looked at him then. Really looked at him. Saw her father's aquiline nose. His stance with the uneven shoulders and bowlegs. How had she missed that at the airport? Shock. Fear. So many reasons.

"You look like him," she said.

"Not that I want to resemble that jerk, but yeah, I do."

"How could you kill him? He was our father."

He narrowed his eyes at her. "How do you know I killed him?"

"I was there. In the building shadows. I saw you shoot him, take the envelope that he tried to give me and then ride right past me."

A shock of surprise lit his face. Then his lip curled like an angry dog. "So he *was* planning to betray me that night. I should have known."

"You said he didn't want to have anything to do with you, but obviously you were connected somehow."

"Yeah, because of his stupidity," Dean snarled.

"Explain, please." She tried to sound calm but her heart was racing as fast as Gavin's stallion could move.

"He abandoned Mom, and me, and we had very little to live on, but we got by. Then when I was in high school, she developed a chronic illness. I had to find a way to provide for us. To pay her medical bills. But how? I was just a kid. So I got involved in dealing drugs." He snorted. "Turns out I was good at it. Worked my way up in the organization. Until I called the shots."

Was he part of the drug syndicate? If so, he was a very dangerous man and she had to be careful not to make him mad. "I'm sorry you had to resort to that, but what does this have to do with killing Dad?"

"My mom said if he'd stuck around, our life would have been easier. I begged her to tell me who he was so I could contact him, but she refused to tell me until she was on her deathbed."

"But why?" Lexie asked as she looked around for any hint of Adam. "He could have helped you."

"Ha! He wouldn't have lifted a finger and she knew that. She said he wouldn't have anything to do with me, and she didn't want me to face rejection on top of being abandoned." His voice caught and he fisted his hands.

At his intensity, Lexie's fears rose.

"She brought him up all the time to tell me how horrible he was so I wouldn't pine for him," Dean continued. "And she was right. He said acknowledging me would ruin him. He couldn't tarnish his precious reputation. I hated him."

"Then why did you contact him?"

"Why?" He sneered. "Because when she died I was left all alone. With no one to rely on but myself. I had to give him a piece of my mind. But you wouldn't understand. He babied you and your brother."

"You don't know what you're talking about! After my mom died, we lived with our aunt and he didn't spend much time with us."

"But he acknowledged you!" He spit on the dirt and ground it in. "That's what he thought of me. Told me to my face." He glared at her as if he was staring right through her.

She didn't want to believe her dad could have been so cruel but losing her mother had changed him. A bitter man, he'd lived for his reputation. And also money, as she'd learned in the last few days. This guy had threatened that, so she could see her father rejecting his son.

A car drove by on the road and Dean snapped out of his trance. "Enough talking. Time to act."

"But you didn't tell me about the syndicate."

"Why would I?"

"So I can understand my father."

A slow, snide smile slid across his lips. "No point. Not when you won't be long for this world."

SEVENTEEN

Gavin wanted to tear open the envelope and read the will, but he set out for the ranch so he wouldn't be gone from Lexie any longer than necessary. Especially with the explosion that had recently occurred on the outskirts of town. His dad would be chomping at the bit to get to the scene, and Gavin didn't blame him.

Eager to see Lexie, he climbed the stairs and pushed open the door. His dad came charging out of the office, his hand on his service weapon. "Good. It's you."

Gavin was thankful his dad was taking Lexie's safety seriously by checking out who was entering the house. Gavin glanced in the family room. Found it empty. "Where's Lexie?"

"She was making coffee and doing the dishes when I last checked on her." He glanced at his watch. "That was about fifteen minutes ago. Been tied up on the phone. I'm sure you've heard about the explosion."

Gavin nodded but his gut felt unsettled. His dad had come running when he'd heard the front door open, but what if someone had come to the door in the kitchen? Would he have heard that from his office?

"I'll just go check on her." Gavin's apprehension got the best of him, so he charged for the kitchen. Found it empty. Spun and returned to the hallway. "She's not in the kitchen."

"Then where…?" His dad's face paled.

"Lexie!" Gavin climbed the stairs two at a time, though he had no reason to suspect she'd be upstairs. "Where are you?"

He glanced into the bathroom then flung open all the bedroom doors. She was nowhere to be found. He bounded back down the stairs. "Not upstairs."

"She could've gone out to the stables," his dad said.

Gavin took off running, calling for her on the way. He heard his father charging after him. Gavin did a quick inventory of horses in the corral. All present and accounted for, and she wasn't anywhere nearby. He fumbled with the latch on the fence and charged into the stable, but quickly determined it was empty.

"Dear God," Gavin prayed in desperation, "where can she be?"

He couldn't stand around to wait for an answer. He raced outside.

"Son?" his father said as he joined him.

Gavin shook his head and couldn't speak aloud the words that Lexie was missing and the killer could have taken her, too.

"Man, oh, man." Looking panic-stricken, his dad started to pace. "How could I have been so *stupid*? I should have been more vigilant. I really let you down."

Gavin opened his mouth to snap at his father as he once would have done, but what good would it do to rail at him? To blame him, when he'd done nothing wrong. Gavin would have let Lexie do the dishes and gone about his own business, too, as the ranch was a secure location. They were all people. Fallible people. This could have happened to any one of them.

He met his dad's distraught gaze. "I'm upset that she's missing, but I understand how it could happen."

Tears filled his dad's eyes. If Lexie wasn't missing, Gavin might say something more, but she was gone. "Pull yourself together, Dad. We have to find her and Adam."

Nodding, his dad squared his shoulders and then clapped him on the back. "We'll find them together, son. You have my word."

"Together," Gavin said, but had no clue where to start.

Gun at her back, Lexie moved deeper onto the property. She needed more information from Dean. Like why he wanted to kill her. Hopefully asking more questions would also distract him long enough to figure out how to get away and free Adam.

"While we walk," she said, "you can at least tell me how my father got involved in the syndicate."

"Our father," he snapped.

She stopped to look back at him. He shoved her and her feet tangled in the long grass. She lost her balance and hit the ground hard. Dean stood over her, sneering, but she wouldn't say a word. She simply got up and straightened her clothes.

"*Our* father," she said. "How did he get involved with the syndicate?"

"Started with him treating me like dirt. Less than dirt. Pond scum. So he had to pay." He gestured with his gun for her to keep moving.

She'd rather watch his face to see his emotional state, but she stared off slowly. "You wanted him dead."

"Not back then, but I did want to see him ruined. To shred the reputation he thought more of than me."

"So you planned to release the DNA results?"

"Are you kidding? That wasn't enough. I wanted him

to beg me to help him first. So I had a colleague sucker him into our Medicaid fraud scheme. He had no idea I was behind it all, and he took the bait. Figured he would, what with his love of money."

"And then you blackmailed him, so he had to peddle your drugs."

Dean laughed. "I wasn't quite ready to reveal myself, but yes, that's exactly what my associate did. Once dear old Dad was in too deep to get out, I made sure he knew I was behind it all. That I now had control over 'his royal highness.'"

He stopped talking and she glanced over her shoulder to see him frowning.

He caught her gaze then pushed her forward as if taking out his anger at their dad on her. How odd it was to think "their dad" and mean someone other than her and Adam. Totally surreal.

"But then Dad took off," she said to keep Dean talking while she looked around for a way to get the drop on him. She caught sight of the old oil tank in the distance, the top removed and a tall ladder on the side. That had to be where he was keeping Adam. She frantically searched for a weapon to use to take Dean out.

"I had to admit I didn't see that happening," he continued on his own, and she listened while surveying the area. "I could never have predicted that he would get a tumor and not have long to live. That he'd want to go somewhere and lick his wounds to die."

So Dad had indeed known he was dying and hadn't told her. "You knew about the cancer?"

"He tried to use it to bargain with me to leave him alone. Didn't believe him until he produced proof. But then he tried to burn me with the syndicate."

"How?" she asked.

"He made me feel like such a loser that I got stupid. Thought if he realized how resourceful and successful I was that I could change his opinion of me. So I bragged about outsmarting the syndicate and skimming money from them. He recorded our conversations and was going to meet with them the day he came back to turn the file over to them."

"Why didn't he do it before he took off? Why wait?"

"He thought if he held on to the tapes that he could control me by threatening to turn me in to the police." Dean's voice vibrated with anger. "He knew I already had two strikes against me and another arrest would put me in prison for a long time. I wasn't going back there."

"It worked, though, didn't it?" She was surprised that she sounded proud of her father's skills when she was beginning to see what a truly unethical man he'd been.

"Until I put all of the syndicate's resources to work and found him." An evil grin slid over his mouth.

"So this envelope contained tapes?" she said, hoping to get all of her questions answered.

"Among other things. Like a mushy letter to you and Adam explaining what he wanted you to do with the tapes."

"Which was what exactly?"

"He admitted that he never was going to turn me in to the police. That would tarnish his reputation. He only wanted to see me pay and figured the syndicate would take care of that." A muscle ticked in Dean's jaw. "So he hired an investigator to follow our delivery mules and figure out my superior's identity."

Just like Lexie suspected. "And did he?"

"Yeah, but he was worried that after he handed over the files, the syndicate would turn on him since he knew their identity, too. And he also thought they might still go after you and Adam."

"But they didn't."

"Only because when he learned he was going to die, he wanted to live out his last months on his own terms, not looking over his shoulder and ending up some syndicate hit. So he held on to the information until nearer his death. Came back to town to give you a copy for leverage against the syndicate."

"I would have turned it over to the police," she said.

"He was banking on your love for Adam to stop you from giving up your insurance and putting his life in jeopardy."

She hadn't thought of that. That was probably what she would have done. Either way, she was thankful she hadn't had to make that decision. Still, it had put her in this situation. Endangered their lives. But why had Dean targeted her?

She stopped walking and faced him. "None of this explains why you abducted me and Adam."

"Why? You want to know why?" His voice rose, stirring birds into flight. "Because even in death he found a way to cheat me out of my rights as his son."

"How?"

"His stinkin' will, that's how. I'm surprised you haven't heard about it yet."

"I don't want his money or things, so I haven't asked to see his will, but how do you know what's in it?"

"He included a copy in the envelope with another stupid explanation for you. Of course he left everything to you and Adam, but he wasn't taking any chances that the syndicate might not get rid of me." Resentment darkened Dean's tone. "He was afraid if I was alive, I could use DNA to prove my parentage and contest the will. So he named your aunt as the estate executor with instructions on how to handle the money. If at any point you could prove I died, the money would be disbursed to you."

She didn't know how to respond, so she said nothing.

He glared at her. "Everything was your fault. If he didn't dote on you so much, he would have spent time with me. He might be dead, but I'm still going to get my revenge."

"How exactly?" she asked.

"You're so stupid you have to ask? How could he have loved you? I'm the superior one. I'm the one he should have loved." He bared his teeth in a snarl. "No matter. You will die today, and I will have the last laugh. Now, get moving before I shoot you without letting you talk to your precious little brother."

"What are you going to do about Adam?" she asked, afraid to hear the answer. If Dean wanted the inheritance, he couldn't possibly leave Adam alive.

"It's not about the money, you know," he said as if reading her thoughts. "It was never about the money. I have plenty. Our snooty father despised Adam as much as me, so I have a soft spot for the kid."

Lexie doubted he had a soft spot for anyone or anything.

"So I don't care what happens to Adam. I didn't let him see my face and didn't tell him my name. Means I can let him go." Dean fixed his gaze on her then fingered one of her curls. "But you, my dear sister, won't make it through the day."

EIGHTEEN

Gavin needed to be in the last place Lexie had been seen. He had no idea why, but he settled in the kitchen and ripped Dr. Grant's will from his pocket to see if it did, in fact, hold a lead.

His dad bustled in the door. "I noticed the truck was gone, so I called your brothers and sisters. None of them took it. Means Lexie must have grabbed the keys from the hook."

"So you think she left of her own volition?"

"Either that or the truck was stolen. Not a likely scenario."

"But why would she leave?" Gavin asked.

"No clue, but I've got Matt requesting a warrant for her phone records. I have to warn you, son, without any sign of a struggle here, we may not get it." He stepped to the back wall and ran his fingers over the key rings dangling on the pegs.

"Keys are gone, all right." His father shook his head. "I should never have let your mother hang them up here. I'm the sheriff, for pity's sake, and know criminals can smash a window and grab them. But with Dad around all the time…" He shrugged. "Still, it's my fault."

"Remember we're not playing the blame game," Gavin

said. "Let's tear into Dr. Grant's will." Letting the envelope flutter to the floor, he started reading, his dad standing behind and peering over his shoulder.

"No way." Gavin pointed at a long clause. "Lexie has a half brother."

"Give me that." Walt grabbed the paper. "Guy's name is Dean Wilcox. Never heard of him."

"Say that again," Gavin said before his mouth dropped open.

"Dean Wilcox. You know the guy?"

"He's one of the cabin guests."

"Here? On my property?" His dad slammed the paper on the table. "How'd I let that happen right under my nose?"

"How could you have known he was a killer?"

"Couldn't have, but still—"

Gavin jumped to his feet. "We need to get over to the cabin. See what we can find."

"I'll grab a set of keys from my office, and I'm right behind you."

At the base of the oil tank, Lexie called out, "Adam, are you in there?"

She thought she heard moaning and reached for the ladder.

"Hold it right there, Lexie," Dean warned. "Your brother's waiting for you, but we need to get you ready first."

She spun. "If he's in there, why didn't he answer?"

"Duct tape. Couldn't have him screaming and alerting anyone who might be brave enough to venture onto the property." He pulled shiny metal handcuffs from his pocket and crossed over to her. "Take off your jacket."

"But why?"

"Just do what I say or I won't release Adam."

She shed her jacket and let it fall to the ground, the cold instantly chilling her body.

"Now, hold out your left wrist."

She complied and he clamped a cuff tight enough to cut off her circulation and bite into her tender flesh. She wanted to cry out, but pressed her lips together so he couldn't see he'd hurt her.

He pulled a ski mask from his pocket and slipped it on. Good. If he continued to hide his face, she'd be seeing Adam soon, and Dean would still let him go.

"Now climb up the ladder and down the one inside." He met her gaze. "Mention my name to Adam and the boy will die right beside you."

Eager to see Adam, she moved fast. She crested the rim and spotted him in good condition minus the tape on his mouth. Her heart soared at seeing him alive and peering up at her, but fell when she noticed his wrists were cuffed to a metal rod that looked something like a towel bar bolted to the wall on both ends.

"Adam," she cried out.

He tried to speak but the tape muffled his words.

She didn't know why he didn't simply slide his hands up the bar to remove the tape. "Take the tape off so I can understand you."

His eyes widened in fear and he shook his head.

"I told him I'd kill you if he did." Dean chuckled as he climbed the ladder.

Adam slid his hands up the pole as if reaching out to her. She hated seeing his desperation. He may be as tall as a full-grown man, but he was still a boy inside. When she got out of this situation, and she would, she'd make sure Dean paid for hurting her brother.

"Get moving, *sis*," Dean said.

She ignored his mocking endearment and maneuvered over the top to the other ladder. On the ground, she grabbed Adam in a hug and kissed his cheek over and over, her helplessness in not being able to free him almost more than she could bear.

"I'm here, bud," she said, making sure she sounded confident. "And I'm going to get us out of this."

"Ha!" Dean peered over the top. "Good luck with that. I've thought of everything." He laughed, the sound reverberating off the walls. "Now, Adam, be a good boy and secure your sister's cuffs to the bar. Make sure it's nice and tight, as I'm going to come down there to check, and if you don't do as I say, she dies."

Tears glistened in Adam's eyes. She didn't want him to have to suffer even more by securing her, so she arranged her hands above his to allow him to easily close the cuff. "It's okay. Do as he says. We'll still find a way out of here."

Adam clamped the cuff, a tear dropping from his cheek onto her arm.

Her anger at Dean mounted. Turned to rage.

She swallowed it down and jerked on her cuffs to show Dean that Adam had followed through. "Ready for your inspection."

He stowed his gun and moved into the tank. Once on the ground, he checked her cuffs.

"What are you going to do with me?" she asked.

"Simple. I'll be filling the tank with water." He backed toward the ladder.

Water? No. He couldn't possibly do that, could he?

"Why go to all this trouble?" she asked. "You've got a gun. Why not just shoot me?"

"Payback. My mother died from lung disease. She struggled to get her breath all the time. I watched her at the end. Her chest convulsing with the need for air. You're going to see what that feels like." His gaze locked on Lexie, hatred and bitterness oozing from his every pore.

"By why this tank?" she asked, hoping to keep him talking to buy time for Gavin to realize she was missing and find her. "It must have taken a long time to make this watertight when a bathtub or lake would have done the same thing."

"You can thank dear old Dad and Grant Oil for that." He sneered. "When Mom told me his name, I couldn't believe it. One of his wells was pumping away on our rental property. Right in the backyard. Day and night, the pump jack's swishing noise nearly drove me crazy."

Nearly?

"Even worse—" he shook his head "—my mother wanted to feel the sun on her face, so we moved her bed by the window. As she suffered, I sat with her and looked out at that pump jack. At the sign boasting Grant Oil. Day after day. Even as she took her last breath, I imagined how wonderful it would be to have the good doctor die in a situation where he couldn't breathe. So I prepared the tank. But he's gone now. My fault. I couldn't control my temper. No matter. You're the sacrificial lamb, and you'll bear the burden of his sins."

Gun in hand, Gavin pushed the door open. Scanned the one-room cabin.

"He's not here." He shoved his gun into the holster and started to enter, but his dad grabbed his arm.

"Let me get gloves and booties from the car so we don't contaminate any evidence."

As much as Gavin wanted to tear the room apart to find a lead, a few seconds to take protective measures for evidence that could help them find Lexie was well worth it.

He snapped on the booties and started prowling the room. "No suitcase or clothes."

"He's taken off."

"Could mean he has Lexie and has no need to come back here."

His dad's jaw clenched. "I'll get Tessa out here to process the space. Maybe she'll find evidence we're missing."

As he called her, Gavin inched through the room, looking for any lead. He spotted a piece of paper in the wastebasket by a small desk and flattened it on the desktop.

"Tessa will be here in less than five," his dad said. "What's that?"

"A receipt. For waterproof caulk. Ten tubes. Bought it at the hardware store in Cumberland five days ago. Paid cash."

"What could he be using all that caulk for?"

Gavin shrugged. "Sealing something. But what?"

"He might own property around here. Let me get Matt to run a background check on Wilcox and see what we can find out about him."

Gavin nodded and returned to his search. He had to find something. Anything to lead them to Lexie. Dear, sweet Lexie. In a killer's hands.

Gavin's heart constricted and he could hardly breathe. Time ticked past. One minute. Two. Five.

Hurry. Hurry. Find something. But what?

Nervous sweat beaded along his neck even in the cold. He heard a car drive up and saw Tessa through the window. He raced to greet her but a drop of liquid near the front door stilled his feet. He squatted to figure out what he was looking at, but his mind was a jumbled mess of fear and panic and he couldn't make sense of the liquid.

"What do you think it is?" his dad asked.

"Looks like oil. But, if so, it's dirty. Like it came from used oil."

"Or crude," Tessa said at the door.

He shot her a look. "If you can tell that from up there, you're better than I thought."

"I wish," she replied. "I got a text on the way over. The oil from the overlook wasn't refined, but crude oil."

A flash of hope took hold in Gavin's heart. "Wilcox could be employed by an oil company. That could be the lead we needed."

His dad shifted his hat. "Makes sense. Those jobs turn over fast, and I can't keep up with the workers coming and going in the county."

Gavin peered at Tessa as he came to his feet. "We found a receipt for ten tubes of waterproof caulk. So where would caulk and crude oil come together?"

"An oil well, I suppose, but surely not with that quantity of caulk."

"Unless he performed maintenance on a large number of wells." Gavin's mind raced over the facts, lighting on them, then spitting them until one held. "You think he took Lexie to a well?"

"If so, we're looking at hundreds of wells in Lake County alone. Not to mention the surrounding counties."

Panic raced along Gavin's nerves and he sought any answer to find her. "These wells just sit out in the open. He'd keep Lexie and Adam in a secluded location."

"Got enough abandoned shacks around here, too," Tessa reminded him.

"Like wells, these shacks are a dime a dozen," his dad said.

"Too many for us to check out in a timely manner." Gavin kicked the doorjamb and thought about slamming a fist into it, as well. He was powerless to help.

How could he have let this happen? How?

His father rested a hand on his shoulder. "That's what family and friends are for, son. We can split up the work and have Lexie home in no time."

Gavin nodded, but they had nearly five hundred square miles of county to cover. How could they possibly do so in a timely basis?

Lexie heard Adam quietly sobbing and could hardly bear his anguish. At least when Dean's task was done, he would let Adam climb out of the tank.

"What good little listeners you are." Dean laughed.

Lexie looked up at him. "Now let Adam go."

He narrowed his eyes. "Um, about that. On second thought, he stays."

"What?" she shouted. "No. You promised."

"I did, didn't I," he said. "But then I saw the torment you felt when you saw him tied up. How much pain will you feel if I leave him behind, too?"

Chuckling, he went for the ladder.

"No! No! Come back here."

He didn't listen but kept moving and cleared the rim. She soon heard water rushing from a three-inch pipe in the wall. At this rate, it wouldn't take long before water covered their heads.

Dear God. Please. I'm begging. If You're there, send Gavin to help us.

NINETEEN

Gavin pressed out a county patrol map on the dining table. He was surrounded by his family minus Matt and Kendall, who were on their way to join everyone at the ranch.

"My deputies know their districts better than we do, so I've already got them looking," his father said. "We'll help search the quadrants that are sparsely populated and too large for one deputy to search."

He picked up a marker and Gavin was thankful for his dad's level head. Gavin wished he was thinking as clearly, but nerves had his hands trembling.

The door opened and he spun to find Matt and Kendall stepping inside.

"Any new info on Wilcox?" Gavin demanded.

"A few things actually," Matt replied.

A tight smile crossed Kendall's mouth. "I got access to Wilcox's credit card account. He's been buying caulk for months from various locations around the area."

His father arched a brow. "I don't want to know how you did that, young lady, but thankfully you did."

"And," Matt added, "Wilcox doesn't work for an oil company. In fact, he has no known source of income, but he's been arrested for possession and intent to sell narcotics."

"Syndicate. Drugs…" Gavin muttered to himself to process. "So why's he tracking crude around on his shoes?"

"That, we don't know."

"He'd have to be stepping all over in it to still be carrying even a trace on his shoes by the time he hit the cabin," Tessa said.

"Probably has rubber mats in the vehicle," Matt said. "If this still has to do with pump jacks, I doubt he'd pick up much near them, as the oil companies are doing a much better job in preventing contamination these days."

"An oil tank," Gavin said.

"You think he has her in a storage tank." Tessa's face paled. "The fumes would—"

"Not a modern metal tank," Gavin interrupted. "But remember that old wooden one that looked like a big wine barrel?"

"The one we wanted to play in when we were kids." Kendall grinned. "And that kid got stuck in the sludge in the bottom."

His dad frowned. "We had to rescue him."

"Is it still standing?" Gavin asked.

"Not sure. I do know the oil company covered it, and we've had no incidents since then."

"It's a perfect place to hide Lexie and Adam, and it could also explain the caulk." Tessa's eyes narrowed. "He could be caulking the slats to make it watertight."

"Because?" Gavin asked, but the answer quickly became clear.

If Gavin didn't get to the tank in time, Wilcox would fill it with water and end Lexie's life.

* * *

Cold water lapped around Lexie's knees and she shivered. How were they going to make it out of the tank alive?

Dean's head poked over the top of the tank. "Good. I see the water is flowing well."

"Please don't do this," Lexie said, her teeth chattering. "At least not to Adam."

"The more you ask me to let him go, the more I want to leave him with you." Dean clapped his hands. "Now, I must go. Your big, bad FBI agent is likely looking for you by now and I don't want to run into any roadblocks."

He disappeared and Adam ripped the tape from his mouth.

"Have you been here all night?" she asked.

He shook his head. "He kept me in some old house with him. So who is he, anyway?"

She quickly explained.

Adam shook his head. "A brother. *Our* brother? Totally freaky."

"We need to let that go for now and get out of here."

"How?"

"Let's start by trying to pull these bars free." She wrapped her hand around a bar so shiny that it had to be newly installed.

"I tried all morning. No luck." Adam held up his wrists covered in angry cuts and bruises.

"I'm so sorry, buddy."

"For what? You didn't do this. It was totally Dad's fault." He sighed and leaned against the wall. "I might still be mad at Gavin, but I would give anything for him to find us."

"You know he has to be searching for us by now."

"Do I?"

"Look," she said and kept trying to wobble the bar holding them captive. "I get it now. He had to leave here or he would die inside." She explained what she'd seen in Gavin and his behavior. "If he'd stayed, he would have been miserable and so would we."

"Fine, but that doesn't mean he couldn't have come back to hang out with me."

"I think he wanted to, but it was too painful for him." She stopped tugging on the bar. "Remember when you and Shelly broke up and how hard it was to see her every day after that. It would have been easier if she'd moved away, right?"

He nodded.

"Well, imagine that when you're all grown up and truly in love. How painful that would be." She peered around the space, looking for a way out while hiding her panic rising as fast as the water.

"Yeah," he said grudgingly.

"Maybe now would be a good time to forgive him," she said not only for Adam but for herself, as well.

"Because we're not getting out of here, you mean?"

"No, because carrying the pain around hurts."

"Sounds like you still love him?"

Did she? She just didn't know. "I'm not sure how I feel about him. Would you hate it if I did love him?"

"I don't know, either," he said. "But I'll think about forgiving him."

She nodded. "Now, how about helping me figure a way out of here?"

"Our only hope is the ladder and we can't even reach that."

He was right. Dean had thought of everything.

"We can pray." She took his hands and offered a prayer,

her eyes filling with tears that she blinked away before Adam saw them.

"God will help, right?" he asked.

She nodded, but one thing she knew for sure. God's help didn't always come in the form you hoped for. If it did, Gavin would be beating a path to them right now.

Come on, Gavin. Please hurry. I need you.

Did it matter that she needed him? Could he get here and free them before the water took her down, or before the cold did them both in?

She jerked on her cuffs again. Shook the bar and started screaming for help until she was hoarse. Adam took over and called out, but the water kept coming. Rising higher. Her thighs. Hips. Waist. Nothing to stop it. She was shorter than Adam, and it reached her chest first. Her heart beat furiously.

"You can float and hook a leg over my shoulder for support," Adam said.

"Just worry about yourself."

"No," he snapped. "I might only be fourteen, but I'm strong and can help you."

"Okay." She hated the thought of him standing in the water alone, but when it hit her chin, she let her body float up to the surface. Lying back, she closed her eyes and prayed again.

"Put your leg over my shoulder," he said.

Lexie didn't want to, as it would hold him down, but it would give him something to concentrate on, so she did. She talked about the future and all the things they had to look forward to to give him hope. He responded, but when the water reached his chest, he stopped talking.

The water would soon reach his mouth, but her hands were fastened above his, so she didn't know if he could float high enough to get his head out of the water. Worse, if she couldn't keep her position she'd drop onto him, and he'd completely sink below the water. And there was no way to change that. No matter how much she loved him and would give her life for him, she couldn't.

She could only trust God now. With the way He didn't seem to hear her, that thought brought little comfort.

Gavin careened the ranch's open-air Jeep around a curve on the narrow road. He and Matt might be safer in his bigger SUV, but the Jeep was a cross-country edition and they'd taken a shortcut to reach the rutted road.

"Careful, bro," Matt said from the passenger seat. "You won't do Lexie any good if you can't get to her."

Panic had his foot pressed to the floor on the straightaway, but Gavin eased up before the next curve. He rounded the bend and a car barreled toward them.

"Watch out!" Matt shouted.

Gavin jerked the wheel to avoid the other vehicle. The Jeep plunged off the road and slammed into a tree. Gavin somehow managed not to hit his head on the dash or windshield.

He shook off the shock. "Are you okay, Matt?"

"Yeah, but no thanks to your lame driving." He unhooked his seat belt and rubbed his chest before climbing out.

Gavin got his belt off, too, and scrambled out of the Jeep and after Matt, who was crossing over to the other vehicle that had run off the road and flipped.

"It's Wilcox," Matt called out.

Gavin's feet stilled. "Is he alive?"

"Yeah, but unconscious, so I can't ask about Lexie and Adam."

"We must have the right location, otherwise why would he be out here?"

"Go after her. But grab the ranch toolbox."

Gavin didn't want to waste time jogging back to the Jeep, but he also didn't want to show up at the oil tank without equipment he might need to rescue them. He clawed through weeds to locate and grab the wayward toolbox. He held it to his chest, allowing him the freedom to run. The weight slowed him down, but he kept going until the oil tank was in view.

"Lexie!" he shouted.

"Gavin!" Her voice came from far off. Had he actually heard it or was it the whistling wind?

He dropped the toolbox and raced for a tall ladder lying on the ground. He heard the hum of a pump in the distance and water running.

"Lexie," he yelled again as he leaned the ladder against the tank.

"In here. We're in here," Adam cried out.

The boy was alive, but what about Lexie? Fear squeezed Gavin's chest as he leaned the ladder against the tank then took the rungs two at a time.

He peered over the top and thought his heart might stop. Adam was cuffed to a long bar and Lexie floated nearby. Her leg hung over Adam's shoulder, the water nearing the teen's chin.

"I'll get you both out of there," Gavin promised. "Just hang on."

She opened her mouth to speak but water threatened and she clamped it closed.

"I'll grab a bolt cutter from the toolbox," Gavin said. "Hold her up, Adam. Please hold her up."

"I've got her."

It took everything Gavin was made of to turn his back on Lexie, but he leaped from the ladder. He hit the ground hard and ran toward a rickety shed where he heard a motor running. He located the water pump near a covered well, going full force, and turned it off to stop the rise of water.

He charged to the toolbox, prayed it held bolt cutters and fought with the rusty old latch. He jerked it open and dumped out the contents, revealing bolt cutters he'd used for years working on the ranch. Back he went toward the tank, pausing to shove his phone into his jacket pocket and shed the coat next to Lexie's, as they would need the warmth once he freed them.

He sped up the ladder. Lexie was sinking. Water lapping at her mouth, her eyes closed.

"Hurry," Adam called.

"Lift her higher," Gavin demanded.

"I can't. I can't." Adam started sobbing, his mouth barely above water.

Gavin wanted to lunge into the water, but he'd create a wave and further swamp them. So he eased down the ladder and into the icy liquid. The cold seeped into his bones and took his breath. They both had to be freezing.

"I turned off the water pump," he said to assure Adam, then felt around for Lexie's wrist. She stirred.

"I've got you, sugar. Cutting off the cuff now."

"Adam first," she mumbled and got a mouth full of water.

She started coughing.

"I'll help Adam next." Gavin found Lexie's handcuff. Sliced through the chain. "Can you put your arms around my neck and hold on while I cut Adam free?"

She tried to lift her arms but was unable to manage. Gavin hated to do it, but he had to let her go to clip Adam's cuffs. He worked fast, but she sank under the water. The moment Adam was free, Gavin reached for her and pushed her head above water.

She coughed and gagged.

"Go," Adam said, his teeth chattering. "Take her out. I'm fine."

Gavin didn't know if the chattering was from the cold or from fear, but in either case, he was right. Gavin had to move Lexie now.

"Get to the ladder and I'll be right back to help you."

"Just make sure Lexie's all right. Okay?"

"You're a good brother, Adam." Gavin made his way to the ladder and shifted her over his shoulder. As he climbed the rungs, he heard her breathing, and his heart sang at the sound. It took him longer than he'd hoped to clear the top and get down to the ground. He gently laid her down and ran for her jacket to drape it over her.

"Adam," she gasped.

"I'm going back for him now." Gavin returned to the tank to find Adam clinging to the ladder.

"Hold your breath," Gavin shouted and plunged from the top.

He got behind Adam and lifted.

Adam started pulling himself up.

"That's it," Gavin encouraged. "You're quite a kid, you know that? You save your sister's life, and you still have something left to climb out of here."

Adam glanced back, pride lighting his face. When he started moving again, he seemed to have more energy, and in short order, they were back on the ground.

Adam glanced around. "Your car. Where is it?"

"I crashed the Jeep about a mile from here. Let's take shelter in the shed, and I'll call for backup. Grab my jacket and put it on."

He scooped Lexie up into his arms and trudged to the dilapidated building that would at least keep them out of the wind. He sat and cradled her on his lap then turned to Adam. "Sit as close to me as possible so we can share body heat."

Adam's whole body trembled as he lowered himself next to Gavin.

Gavin fished his phone from his jacket pocket and dialed Matt to fill him in and request an ambulance.

"Already called one," Matt said. "Dad should be here ASAP, too."

"Wilcox alive?"

"Yeah."

"Good," Gavin said. He wanted the man to live so he could spend the rest of his life behind bars to pay for his crimes.

Gavin stowed his phone and slung his arm around Adam. He pulled both of them closer and offered a prayer of thanks. God had been there. With him all this time. He got that now and understood that, no matter how many times he'd asked God to change his circumstances since Emily had been shot, the point was for God to leave him in his mess to work through his own problems and change him along the way. He was changed now. For good. His priorities were finally straight.

"I made a big mistake when I left both of you," he said fervently. "Can you forgive me?"

"I can," Adam said.

Gavin knuckled his head and peered at him. "Thanks, bud. You know I love you, don't you?"

"Yeah," he said, now sounding embarrassed.

Gavin turned his attention to Lexie. She was looking at him, but her gaze seemed far away. He pressed a kiss to her forehead and stroked her cheek. "Did you hear me, sugar?"

"Yes," she said, but then closed her eyes and didn't continue speaking.

Gavin's heart split. Had he waited too long to realize he couldn't live without her and now she was unable to forgive him? If so, he'd do everything he could to change her mind.

"I'm never leaving the two of you again." He tightened his hold on them. "I'll find a way to make things work with us," he promised, but Lexie's eyes remained closed.

He had no idea if she'd even heard him, much less wanted a future with him, but he wouldn't give up.

EPILOGUE

Lexie unloaded the dishwasher in Ruth's kitchen and glanced at the clock. Eleven fifty-five. In precisely five minutes, the doorbell would ring and, as much as she wanted to avoid it, her heart clutched at the thought of seeing her daily visitor.

She dried her hands and went to the foyer, where she'd placed a small wooden storage box with twelve slots. Eleven slots held Christmas tree ornaments depicting the Twelve Days of Christmas. For the last eleven days at precisely twelve o'clock, Gavin rang the doorbell to pick Adam up to take him on a fun outing. Gavin also gave her an ornament and reminded her that she was his one and only true love, and he was one day closer to living in Lost Creek.

He'd reconciled with his father, but didn't think they should work together, so he'd left the FBI to take a job with the Texas Rangers' division of the Texas Department of Public Safety in Austin, which was within commuting distance to Lost Creek. He also offered the promise that he would never give up on their being together. And each day that he arrived with an ornament and proclaimed his love, her heart let go of a bit of the hurt his abandonment had caused. With today being Christmas

Eve and day twelve of his ritual, she had no idea what he planned next. She had to admit she was eager to see.

The bell chimed and her heart lurched in anticipation. She opened the door and her eyes drank in the sight of him looking so ruggedly handsome in his jeans, boots and cowboy hat. He held out his hand, revealing a delicate glass figurine of a drummer in a red uniform with a silver drum. She took the ornament and held her breath in wait for his next words.

"As of this moment, I am no longer an FBI agent, and I have submitted my change of address to the Lost Creek post office," he said. "Means we're neighbors again, sugar, but I'd like it to be much more."

"Gavin, I—"

He tipped her chin up with one finger and stared deep into her eyes. "I love you, Lexie, and I hope you'll consider giving me a second chance."

Her heart told her to trust him. To throw herself into his arms. But her brain warned her that he'd once promised a future with her and then left her behind.

What was it going to take to convince her to give him a chance? Could she even do so?

"I want to but…" She felt the urging to give in but she held her ground.

His smile vanished. "What's it going to take for you to trust me again?"

'I don't know."

"But you do think you'll get there, right?"

"I don't know that, either."

He took a long breath and blew it out, his gaze filled with angst that tore at her heart.

"You know I'll never give up until you, me and Adam are a family, don't you?"

"I know that's what you want now, but will you still want it tomorrow? Or next year."

He pressed his forehead against hers and she was powerless to move.

"I have never known anything was more right in my life and I will never leave you again. Never. You hear me, Lex. Never."

She wanted to melt closer. Fall into his arms. The pain of his abandonment was gone, but the fear of him going again had a strong grip on her and she couldn't say yes.

Adam stepped into the foyer, holding a basketball and keeping her from having to answer.

He glanced between them. "She said no again, huh?"

"Basically," Gavin said, disappointment crowning in his voice. "But I still want to invite the two of you and Ruth to come to church with us tonight and then have a late supper with my family."

Adam faced her. "Can we go? Please?"

She may not be ready to commit to Gavin, but Adam wanted Gavin in his life and she didn't want to stand in his way. "I'll think about it."

His happy expression fell and she almost caved on the spot, but she really did have to think about whether she was ready to be a part of the McKade family if only for a night.

"C'mon, bud." Gavin knuckled Adam's head. "Time for me to skunk you in b-ball."

They departed, and as tears flooded Lexie's eyes, she settled the ornament in the case. She ran her fingers over each one, thinking about what it meant to be someone's true love. Gavin was hers. She knew that and wanted nothing more than to be with him forever. But…

She closed the box and felt as if she was closing the door on their relationship. Tears started falling in earnest now. She heard footsteps behind her and turned to find Ruth.

"The last ornament?" she asked.

Lexie nodded.

"And now you're crying." Ruth shook her head. "You know I've stayed out of this, but I can't any longer. I understand your pain, and see how you can't trust him. He hurt you, and you've gone through so much to get your life back. But, honestly, I don't think you ever made it back to normal. You've been reliving the pain over and over, right?"

Lexie nodded.

"Then let me tell you what my daddy once told me. Bad things happen to good people. It's a given. But it takes a smart person to know when and how to let it go. You're smart, Lex. You have to see how Adam has blossomed with Gavin back in his life, and I know you can, too. Trust God. Let this go."

Her words hit Lexie in a way she hadn't experienced so far. Even if she forgave Gavin, and he left her in torment again, she was already in torment without him, so why not give him a chance? Why not blossom as Ruth had said? Trust God to have her back in this. He'd been there for her at the oil tank. Saved her and put Dean behind bars to stand trial. God could handle this, too.

"Gavin invited the three of us to go to church and have dinner with his family tonight. I'd like for us to go."

"Of course, sweetheart." Ruth gathered Lexie in a hug. "I can think of no better way to spend Christmas Eve."

A huge burden lifted from Lexie's shoulders and, later in the day, her heart filled to brimming when she told Adam they were going. She made him promise not to tell Gavin, as she wanted it to be a surprise. She spent the rest of the day choosing an outfit, taking a long bath and then dressing for the night.

When they arrived at the small white church on a hill in the country, she was nearly breathless with excitement. The air still held a nip and her bare legs beneath the flowing skirt of her red dress were chilled, so she hurried up the steps.

The pastor greeted them at the door and she eagerly stepped inside the foyer to inhale the fragrance of pine from strung garland and a towering tree with white decorations. She quickly spotted the McKade family settling into their usual pew at the front. Gavin, still standing, glanced back and caught sight of her, stilling in place.

They stood there unmoving, locked in each other's gazes. For how long, she didn't know, but when his family members all turned to stare at her, she came to her senses. His mother reached up and clutched his arm, a wide smile crossing her face.

He started down the aisle toward Lexie, but she couldn't move.

Ruth cleared her throat. "Adam and I'll take a seat."

Gavin passed them in the aisle, his smile lighting up as he gave Adam a playful punch. Adam threw his arms around Gavin and hugged him.

Tears came to Lexie's eyes. Glorious, happy tears.

They parted and Adam continued down the aisle.

"You came," he said gruffly.

She nodded.

"Does this mean—?"

"I forgive you and want us to be together. Yes, that's exactly what it means."

"I love you, Lexie." He pulled her into his arms and twirled.

"I love you, Gavin," she whispered. "You're my one true love, too."

He suddenly stopped and lowered his head. She knew he was going to kiss her, but then he tipped his head at his family. "We have quite the audience."

"I suspect we're going to have the same audience in this very place when you kiss me on our big day."

"Yes, but I want privacy for this." He clutched her hand and led her outside and around the building.

His lips pressed against hers, the kiss urgent and fraught with emotion. She flung her arms around his neck to draw him closer and deepen the kiss, her heart bursting with happiness.

Peace settled over her. God's peace and peace in her core for the first time since her mother had died. Today was the beginning of a new life. She had her brother and Ruth, and now the entire McKade clan, to call family. What could be more right?

Gavin lifted his head, his boyish grin on his face. "I can assure you that no matter the plans you, Ruth, Nana and Mom get up to, I'm putting my foot down now. Our big day won't be in the distant future. Not distant at all."

"No worries, cowboy." She ran her fingers over the solid planes of his face. "I've thought about our wedding so many times, I can plan it in my sleep and I'll have you down that aisle before you know what hit you."

* * * * *

*If you enjoyed this story, don't miss the action-packed
books from Susan Sleeman's most recent miniseries,*
FIRST RESPONDERS:

*SILENT NIGHT STANDOFF
EXPLOSIVE ALLIANCE
HIGH-CALIBER HOLIDAY
EMERGENCY RESPONSE
SILENT SABOTAGE
CHRISTMAS CONSPIRACY*

Find more great reads at www.LoveInspired.com

Dear Reader,

There's nothing I like more than starting a new series and I hope you enjoyed the first book in my McKade Law miniseries. This family is like so many I met in the time I lived in Texas. Hardworking. Honest and God-fearing. And yet their lives are invaded with turmoil and challenges just like yours and mine, and their faith is tested.

In this story, Lexie feels abandoned and unloved. Gavin feels misunderstood and guilty. Yet, through it all, they recognize the strength and compassion of the McKade family, and both long to be part of this strong family unit once again. I hope that you will enjoy getting to know the McKades and enjoy all four books with this family as much as I am enjoying writing them.

If you'd like to learn more about my other books, please stop by my website at www.susansleeman.com. I also love hearing from readers, so please contact me via email at susan@susansleeman.com, on my Facebook page, www.facebook.com/SusanSleemanBooks, or write to me c/o Love Inspired, HarperCollins 24th floor, 195 Broadway, New York, NY 10007.

Susan Sleeman

COMING NEXT MONTH FROM
Love Inspired® Suspense

Available January 2, 2018

SHATTERED LULLABY
Callahan Confidential • by Laura Scott

On the run with her baby nephew after overhearing her sister's murder, Lacy Germaine's suspicious of everyone—including the K-9 officer who saves her from a gunman. But with an elusive enemy threatening her, she needs Matthew Callahan's help to survive.

THE BABY ASSIGNMENT
The Baby Protectors • by Christy Barritt

Tasked with figuring out who left a baby at the Houston FBI office, Special Agent Tanner Wilson has only one clue—his ex-girlfriend's name written on a scrap of paper. But Macy Mills doesn't recognize the little girl, and soon someone's dead set on abducting her...even if it costs Tanner's and Macy's lives.

DUTY TO DEFEND
by Jill Elizabeth Nelson

Working undercover at a day care with child-advocate attorney Jax Williams, Deputy Marshal Daci Marlowe has one mission: protect a woman and her infant son from her fugitive ex-boyfriend. But when the man seems more focused on killing Daci, she and Jax have to figure out why...before it's too late.

DEADLY EXCHANGE
by Lisa Harris

When one of the girls she rescued goes missing and her father's kidnapped, trauma specialist Kayla Brooks is sure *she's* the human traffickers' next target. Her only ally is former Army Intelligence Officer Levi Cummings. But after she helped put his brother in prison, can she trust him with her life?

MISSION: MEMORY RECALL
Rangers Under Fire • by Virginia Vaughan

Trying to uncover the truth about the disappearance and presumed death of army ranger Marcus Allen—the man she loved—CIA Analyst Bethany Bryant discovers he's alive and may be a traitor. But Marcus claims he doesn't remember her or his past...and now someone wants them both dead.

MOJAVE RESCUE
by Tanya Stowe

Kidnapped for her weapons plans, warfare engineer Drina Gallagher believes there's no hope of escape—until undercover CIA agent Cal Norwood blows his cover to save her. But can they survive a chase across the Mojave Desert?

LOOK FOR THESE AND OTHER LOVE INSPIRED BOOKS WHEREVER BOOKS ARE SOLD, INCLUDING MOST BOOKSTORES, SUPERMARKETS, DISCOUNT STORES AND DRUGSTORES.

LISCNM1217

Get 2 Free Books,
Plus 2 Free Gifts—
just for trying the *Reader Service!*

LIS17R2

SPECIAL EXCERPT FROM

Love Inspired.
SUSPENSE

Special Agent Tanner Wilson has only one clue to figure out who left a baby at the Houston FBI office—his ex-girlfriend's name written on a scrap of paper. But Macy Mills doesn't recognize the little girl that someone's determined to abduct at any cost.

Read on for a sneak preview of
THE BABY ASSIGNMENT *by* **Christy Barritt***,*
available January 2018 from Love Inspired Suspense!

Suddenly, Macy stood. "Do you smell that, Tanner?"

Smoke. There was a fire somewhere. Close.

"Go get Addie," he barked. "Now!"

Macy flew up the steps, urgency nipping at her heels.

Where there was smoke, there was fire. Wasn't that the saying?

Somehow, she instinctively knew that those words were the truth. Whoever had set this fire had done it on purpose. They wanted to push Tanner, Macy and Addie outside. Into harm. Into a trap.

As she climbed higher, she spotted the flames. They licked the edges of the house, already beginning to consume it.

Despite the heat around her, ice formed in her gut.

She scooped up Addie, hating to wake the infant when she was sleeping so peacefully.

Macy had to move fast.

She rushed downstairs, where Tanner waited for her. He grabbed her arm and ushered her toward the door.

Flames licked the walls now, slowly devouring the house. Tanner pulled out his gun and turned toward Macy.

She could hardly breathe. Just then, Addie awoke with a cry.

The poor baby. She had no idea what was going on. She didn't deserve this.

Tanner kept his arm around her and Addie.

"Let's do this," he said. His voice held no room for argument.

He opened the door. Flames licked their way inside.

Macy gasped as the edges of the fire felt dangerously close. She pulled Addie tightly to her chest, determined to protect the baby at all costs.

She held her breath as they slipped outside and rushed to the car. There was no car seat. There hadn't been time.

Instead, Macy continued to hold Addie close to her chest, trying to shield her from any incoming danger or threats. She lifted a quick prayer.

Please help us.

As Tanner started the car, a bullet shattered the window.

Don't miss
THE BABY ASSIGNMENT by Christy Barritt,
available January 2018 wherever
Love Inspired® Suspense books and ebooks are sold.

LISEXP1217

Inspirational Romance to
Warm Your Heart and Soul

Join our social communities to connect
with other readers who share your love!

Sign up for the Love Inspired newsletter
at **www.LoveInspired.com** to be the
first to find out about upcoming titles,
special promotions and exclusive content.

CONNECT WITH US AT:

Harlequin.com/Community

 Facebook.com/LoveInspiredBooks

 Twitter.com/LoveInspiredBks

LISOCIAL2017